Leigh Michaels has written almost seventy novels for Harlequin Romance®. Her sparkling, warmly emotional style has captivated readers around the world, and she has over thirty million books in print. Translated into more than twenty languages, her stories feature characters that women everywhere, from all nationalities, can relate to—and enjoy reading time and again!

For fresh, emotionally exhilarating novels, look out for Leigh Michaels!

Don't miss Leigh's next book:
Bride by Design
On sale October 2002 (#3720)

Leigh loves to hear from her readers. You can write to her at P.O. Box 935, Ottumwa, Iowa, 52501-0935, U.S.A. Or e-mail: leighmichael@franklin.lisco.net.

Books by Leigh Michaels

HARLEQUIN ROMANCE®
3628—THE CORPORATE WIFE
3637—THE BRIDAL SWAP
3656—A CONVENIENT AFFAIR
3672—HIS TROPHY WIFE
3691—BACKWARDS HONEYMOON

From boardroom...to bride and groom!

**A secret romance, a forbidden affair,
a thrilling attraction?**

Working side by side, nine to five—and beyond....
No matter how hard these couples try
to keep their relationships strictly professional,
romance is definitely on the agenda!

But will a date in the office diary
lead to an appointment at the altar?
Find out in this exciting new miniseries
from Harlequin Romance®.

Look out for
A Professional Marriage (#3721)
by Jessica Steele
On sale October 2002

THE BOSS'S DAUGHTER
Leigh Michaels

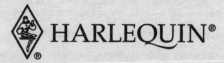

TORONTO • NEW YORK • LONDON
AMSTERDAM • PARIS • SYDNEY • HAMBURG
STOCKHOLM • ATHENS • TOKYO • MILAN • MADRID
PRAGUE • WARSAW • BUDAPEST • AUCKLAND

ISBN 0-373-03711-2

THE BOSS'S DAUGHTER

First North American Publication 2002.

Copyright © 2002 by Leigh Michaels.

Visit us at www.eHarlequin.com

Printed in U.S.A.

CHAPTER ONE

AMY hesitated outside her father's hospital room. Then she took a deep breath and pushed the door open. No matter what Gavin Sherwood wanted to tell her, she knew that delaying wouldn't make it any easier to take, so she might just as well get it over with.

Inside the room, she paused to look at the man lying propped up in the hospital bed, surrounded by high-tech equipment. There was less machinery now than there had been three days ago, when she'd seen him in the intensive care unit right after his heart attack. He was still very ill, there was no denying that. But his color was better, and he was no longer nearly as fragile-looking as he had been a few days before. He was going to make it.

So whatever Gavin had on his mind, Amy told herself, she would listen patiently and politely and then do precisely as she pleased. She wouldn't exactly blow a raspberry at him, of course, no matter what he said—because he was still her father. But she wasn't going to be manipulated into making any deathbed promises to a man who clearly wasn't on his deathbed.

Gavin opened his eyes. ''You finally got my message, I see.''

He sounded a little querulous, Amy thought, and his voice hadn't yet regained all its power—or perhaps the feeble quaver was intentional.

Amy moved closer to the bedside. ''Message? It sounded more like a summons to me.''

"Took you long enough to get here. Where have you been? Out all night?"

As if he has any right to ask. "No, I got up early and went out for a walk. What is it you want, Gavin?"

"It's a bit involved, I'm afraid. Sit down, Amy."

"No, thanks. I didn't come for a leisurely chat, and I'd just as soon not be here when your fiancée gets back from the cafeteria or wherever she's gone."

"Honey went home for a while."

Amy lifted an eyebrow. *So she could rest, or so you could?* she wanted to ask.

"This has been an ordeal for her."

"She was obviously under a lot of stress the night you came into the hospital," Amy agreed. *In fact, she seemed to regard your illness as a great personal inconvenience.*

"She's very young," Gavin Sherwood said quietly. "She's never faced serious illness before in anybody she truly cares about."

And perhaps she still hasn't. Amy's tongue was getting sore from biting it, but she knew better than to say what she thought. Her father was already quite aware that his soon-to-be trophy wife was a major thorn in his daughter's side, so it was unnecessary—and hardly sporting—for Amy to take cheap shots at Honey's expense. Even more important, if she kept criticizing Honey, her opposition would only drive Gavin into defending his choice, further deepening the chasm between father and daughter.

But as long as Honey wouldn't be popping in at any moment, she might as well make herself comfortable, Amy decided, and pulled up a chair. "So what did you want to talk to me about? The message you left on my answering machine wasn't exactly chatty."

"The nurses were hanging around when I called. How's the job hunt coming along?"

"Quite well, thanks. Which I could have told you on the phone. So why was it so important that I drive over here?"

Gavin's fingers plucked at the sheet. "My doctor says I can be released from the hospital in a few days. But of course I'm still facing a long recovery. I won't be able to do much for myself at first."

"I'm sure Honey will make a terrific nurse," Amy said firmly. "It'll give her a preview of the real meaning of 'for better or for worse.' And she looks stunning in white."

"That's not what I'm concerned about. Of course she'll be there for me."

I hope you're right, Amy wanted to say.

"It's the auction house, you see. My doctor says I can't go back to work for several weeks, so someone will have to step in, and of course you're the obvious choice..." His voice trailed off as he looked up at her.

Amy was already shaking her head, and her voice was steady. "I don't work there anymore, Gavin. Remember?"

"Officially you're still on a leave of absence, you know."

"I told you I quit, and I meant it. It was your choice not to accept my resignation."

Gavin didn't seem to hear her. "And if it hadn't been for that silly misunderstanding, you would still be there. So it's only sensible that you come back and—"

"*Silly misunderstanding?* I walked into your office and found you on the couch with Honey, and you call it a silly misunderstanding?"

"Of course you were upset, Amy."

"Darn right I was. Remember? That was the first clue I had that you were planning to divorce my mother."

"I know. And I truly wish you hadn't found out that way."

"That," Amy said tersely, "makes two of us."

"But to actually leave your job, to turn your back on the family business, over something like that... Honestly, Amy, now that you've had a chance to cool off and think it over, don't you agree that you were being a little excessive?"

Amy considered. "Yes," she said finally. "I *was* a little excessive. I should have gone back to my desk and written you a polite resignation letter instead of screaming 'I quit!' at the top of my lungs in the middle of the executive suite while Honey was still trying to get her sweater back on. My technique left a lot to be desired, I admit—put it down to the shock of the situation. But if you're asking whether I have regrets over my decision—no, I don't. After a display of that sort of bad judgment, I'd have trouble trusting any boss."

Gavin looked at her shrewdly. "You can't expect me to believe that you don't miss the auction house."

He was right about that, Amy conceded. She couldn't honestly say that she didn't miss Sherwood Auctions. She'd worked in her father's business, in one capacity or another, ever since she could remember. Before she was a teenager, she'd been running errands, cleaning offices, watching the cloakroom. Later she'd moved up to writing catalog copy, spotting bids during auctions, and researching merchandise. And as soon as she had her degree she'd joined the full-time staff, though she'd still moved from department to department—taking a hand wherever she was needed.

Leaving a firm which had occupied so much of her

life wouldn't have been easy under any circumstances, but that fact didn't mean she was sorry she'd done it. Once she was finally settled in a new job, she'd be contented again.

"It was time for a change, and I'm looking forward to new challenges." She knew she sounded evasive.

Gavin bored in. "Doing what?"

"I'm not absolutely certain yet. But just because I haven't accepted a job doesn't mean I don't have any prospects."

"But the bottom line is that you're still out of work," Gavin mused. "Even after more than two months of looking."

"Blame yourself for that, because you paid me well enough that I could take my time and look around instead of jumping at the first possibility. And if you're speculating on why no one seems to want me—as a matter of fact, it looks as if I'm going to have three different offers any day now. Good offers, too. I'll have a hard time figuring out which one I want to take."

Gavin said slowly, "And each of them will give you a big change and a new challenge? Is that really what you want, Amy?"

"Yes, it is. I'm sorry, but—" She could afford to be gentle, now that he finally seemed to be hearing her.

"That's exactly why you should come back and run the auction house instead," Gavin pointed out brightly. "That'll be a big change and a new challenge, too, because you've always worked in the separate departments. You've never before tried being in charge of everything."

"And that's why I'm the wrong person for the job. You've got a personal assistant who already oversees all the details. Why not promote him?"

"His name isn't Sherwood."

"So maybe he'll change it if you ask him nicely."

Gavin looked at her narrowly. "You still haven't forgiven me for hiring Dylan instead of giving you the job, have you, Amy?"

"Where did you get that delusion? I didn't want to be a glorified secretary, making phone calls and excuses."

"Dylan is not a glorified secretary."

"Great. If he's been so involved in the business, he's capable of taking over for a while. I don't know why you wanted a personal assistant in the first place if you aren't going to use him to advantage."

"Dylan is very good," Gavin said, but Amy thought the tone of his voice sounded far less certain than the words. "But you know how personal the auction business is. It's a matter of trust, and I've worked for decades to build up that trust. My clients trust Sherwood Auctions because they trust me."

"So if you're saying that no one can take your place, Gavin, what's the point of asking me to try?"

"Because the next best thing to the Sherwood they're familiar with is a different Sherwood. It's just the same as when my father handed the business down to me, back when we were still selling farm machinery and odds and ends instead of antiques and fine art. His clients were willing to give me a try, because I was his son. And you don't only have the name, Amy, and the instincts—you've got twenty years of experience in the business."

"Only if you count when I was six years old and I handed out catalogs to bidders as they came into the auctions," Amy muttered. "I had to stand on a chair."

Gavin smiled. "And our auctions in those days were

still small enough that a child could handle the weight of a stack of catalogs.''

''Nostalgia is not going to change my mind, Gavin. Give your personal assistant a chance. If this hadn't happened, you'd have counted on him to keep the place running while you were on your honeymoon. What's so different about letting him take over now? It's just a little longer, that's all.'' Amy stood up and firmly changed the subject. ''Speaking of honeymoons, is the date firm yet? Though I suppose it would be chancy to choose a day for the wedding before the divorce is final.''

Gavin didn't seem to hear her. His hand went out to clutch at her sleeve. ''All right. I didn't want to tell you this, Amy, but I suppose I don't have a choice.''

Now what was he going to try? Hadn't he already run the gamut of persuasive techniques?

''You know, of course, about the financial settlement your mother and I have agreed to as part of the divorce.''

''I know you made an agreement,'' Amy said slowly. ''She didn't give me the details, and I didn't think it was any of my concern as long as Mother was satisfied.''

''Well, that's the problem, you see. She may not be satisfied for much longer.''

Amy sat down again. ''Perhaps you'd better take this from the top, Gavin.''

''We agreed to split our assets as equally as possible. After being married so many years, I felt it was the only arrangement that was fair to Carol.''

''Also the only arrangement she'd have accepted, considering that you were the one who wanted out of the marriage,'' Amy said, almost under her breath.

''But it was impossible to split everything straight down the middle. For instance, Carol wanted the house and I—of course—wanted to keep the business. But because the values of those two things weren't anywhere near equal, I agreed to make her a lump sum payment as compensation for her share of Sherwood Auctions. It's quite a large amount, and it's due pretty soon.''

''If you're threatening to withhold that payment unless I cooperate,'' Amy said, ''you'd better think again.''

''I'm not trying to blackmail you, Amy.'' Gavin fidgeted a little. ''The fact is I can't pay Carol, because I don't have the money. My expenses these last few months have been heavier than I anticipated. All the attorneys' fees, you know…. I've ended up paying your mother's as well as my own, and the legal bills are still coming in. And of course it isn't cheap setting up a new apartment from scratch.''

''To say nothing of the cost of tickets for a honeymoon in Italy,'' Amy agreed. *Poor Daddy—Honey's obviously been a lot more expensive than you anticipated.*

''It isn't as if I haven't been working on it,'' Gavin said. He sounded almost defensive. ''There are a number of potential clients I've been working on for some time. You know the routine, Amy—it takes people time to decide to part with treasures they've collected. Time, and gentle handling, because they have to be comfortable with the decision. I was planning to see several of those people again in the next couple of weeks because I think they're ready to confirm some deals. But then this happened.'' He waved a hand at the machinery that surrounded him. ''And I'm stuck.''

''I don't suppose you'll be making any goodwill calls for a while,'' Amy agreed.

''Without the personal approach, those people are likely to change their minds altogether, or else take their business to another auction house. I can't really blame them for thinking that they might not get the kind of

attention at Sherwood that they would if I was there.''
He shot a sideways look at her. ''Unless you take over,
Amy. Because you're my heir, you see, the reputation
of the firm is just as important to you as it is to me, so
you'll work just as hard to uphold it.''

''Or at least the clients will believe that,'' Amy murmured. ''How could they possibly know the truth?—that
Dylan is probably a lot more concerned about the reputation of the auction house than I am. It's his bread and
butter, after all—not mine. Not anymore.''

''You already know, Amy, that perception is everything in this business. What the clients believe is important. And in any case, it's true—you've lived and
breathed the auction business all your life, my dear, and
whatever you say, you don't want to see it destroyed.
All I'm asking is a few more weeks. And it's really more
for your mother's sake than mine.''

Cunning of him, to put it that way. Amy shrugged.
''Now that's a thought. You could just turn the business
over to Mother for a while. After all, she's lived and
breathed it even longer than I have, and with her financial future at stake—''

Gavin's eyebrows tilted. ''You're joking, surely.''

''Well, yes, I suppose I am,'' Amy admitted. ''But
couldn't you just talk to her? Explain what's happened?''

Gavin shook his head. ''I can't see her being very
understanding. And I can't blame her, exactly—I got
myself into this predicament.''

He was no doubt right about his soon-to-be-ex-wife's
lack of sympathy, Amy thought. Who could blame Carol
Sherwood for still being furious over her ex-husband's
behavior? Amy didn't think her mother would actually
be shortsighted enough to put revenge ahead of her own

financial interests. But Amy could understand why Gavin was hesitant to confess his predicament to Carol. If she did become vindictive, she'd be within her rights to demand her money even if it required Gavin to liquidate everything he owned, and he didn't want to take the slightest chance of having that happen.

"And postponing the payment for a few weeks wouldn't help much anyway," Gavin said heavily, "if the business I've cultivated so carefully goes somewhere else in the meantime."

Amy sighed. "All right. I'll see what I can do."

Gavin gripped her hand. "That's my girl," he said. "I knew I could count on you."

Amy paused for a full fifteen seconds on the sidewalk, looking up at the block-square brown-brick building—originally a warehouse—that housed her father's auction business, before she took a deep breath and pulled open the main door.

It had been nearly three months since she had set foot inside Sherwood Auctions, and just an hour ago, she'd have sworn that she would never walk through those doors again. But here she was anyway—pretty much resigned to the fact, if not precisely happy about it.

She stopped in the small entrance lobby. The half-dozen comfortable chairs opposite the reception desk were all empty, but that wasn't unusual. It wasn't exactly early, but the auction business didn't really get moving till at least the middle of the day.

Behind the reception desk, a man in a dark suit was on the telephone, obviously scheduling an appointment for the caller with one of the auction house's expert appraisers. That might take a while, Amy knew. Though she tapped the toe of her sandal on the marble floor, the action was more to give her something to do than because she was feeling impatient.

"Mrs. Gleason will see you on Thursday morning at ten," the man at the desk said. "Thank you for calling Sherwood Auctions, Mrs. Carter." He stood up. "Good morning. How may I help—" His question broke off abruptly as he got a good look at Amy, and he went on disbelievingly, "Ms. Sherwood?"

She didn't blame him for being startled. "In the flesh, Robert."

"But your father isn't—" He sounded a bit apprehensive. "I mean, you do know about…don't you?"

"About his heart attack? Relax, I haven't been that far out of the loop. I just came from seeing him in the hospital. I'm here because…" She paused. *Because I'm taking over.* She hadn't even said it out loud to herself, and at the last moment she realized she couldn't get her tongue around the words to explain it to anyone else just yet. Not till she'd had a little more time to get used to the idea herself. So instead of telling Robert the truth, she said, "Because I need to see Beth Gleason. Has she come in yet?"

Robert nodded. "Go on up, Ms. Sherwood." He pushed a button on the desk and the inner door unlocked with a soft buzz.

Amy was just a little startled that he hadn't phoned Beth to come down to greet her. No one but the staff was supposed to wander around the building without an escort. In fact, considering the way Amy had departed almost three months ago, she wouldn't have been too surprised if instead of casually letting her enter, Robert had vaulted the reception desk, seized her by the neck, and thrown her out onto the street. Even if her father had sentimentally left her name on the employee roster, the rest of the staff had to know the truth.

Amy stepped through the doorway and into the main lobby. While the reception area was elegant in a very understated way, the two-story-high lobby on the other side of the locked door—where no client or bidder or visitor ever went without an escort—had been deliberately designed to overwhelm. Though it contained nothing but a branching staircase with a cloakroom tucked underneath and a matched pair of elevators, the room often drew gasps from the first-time visitor. Quite an understandable reaction, Amy had always thought, since the staircase had been salvaged from a centuries-old manor house, the linen-fold paneling which covered the elevator doors from a minor palace, and the arched ceiling from a small cathedral. None of them were the sort of thing often seen in Kansas City.

Perception is everything in this business, Gavin had said, and he was right. It had cost him a fortune to create the image of a solid, wealthy, timeless business, but the investment had more than paid for itself. When clients who had been doubtful about what to do with their treasures saw this lobby, they abruptly relaxed, certain that they and their possessions were in good hands. Amy had seen it happen a hundred times.

She could have taken the elevator from the lower lobby all the way to the top of the building where the executive offices were located, but she much preferred to climb the stairs as far as she could. She liked to let her hand trail along the satin-smooth railing as she climbed, liked to see the view from the top step as a second and even larger lobby opened out in front of her. To one side, across what seemed an acre of carpet, was a pillared archway leading into the auction room where the rare and unusual items that were Sherwood Auctions' specialty were put under the hammer. On the other side of the lobby, smaller doors led into a series of museum-like showrooms where prospective buyers could inspect the merchandise days or even weeks before the actual auction.

This morning the auction room was empty and the showrooms quiet. Amy paused just long enough to glance into the showrooms before she went on upstairs. The next scheduled auction, she concluded, must be furniture, for a classic highboy occupied the place of honor just inside the main showroom.

Upstairs, where the clients seldom came, the image of ancient success abruptly gave way to practicality. The fourth floor was a warren of offices, storage closets, and workrooms; she walked down two long corridors before stopping to tap at the door of a cramped office. A young woman wearing a lab coat and white cotton gloves looked up from a china figurine standing on her desk, her mouth dropping open as she saw Amy.

"Sevres?" Amy asked, pointing at the figurine.

Beth Gleason stripped off her gloves. "No. Unfortunately, it's just a darn good imitation."

"And now you have to break the news to the owner, who expected to make a small fortune on it?"

"My favorite part of the job," Beth said dryly. "What are you doing here? You told me you'd only come back over your father's..." Her voice trailed off. "Sorry. That's not very funny just now."

"Well, he's not dying. In fact, for a guy who had a heart attack just a few days ago, he's looking incredibly good." Amy brushed packing fibers off a chair and sat down. "He wants me back on the payroll, only this time I'm supposed to run the whole show."

"Take Gavin's place? For how long?"

"Until he's able to work again. A few weeks, he said."

Beth picked up a box and nestled the pseudo-Sevres figurine into it. "It makes a lot of sense," she said slowly.

Amy's jaw dropped. "From whose point of view? I've spent more than two months cultivating new job possibilities, but now that I'm finally getting nibbles you think I should be pleased about turning them all down so I can fill in for my father?"

"If the people who have offered you jobs really want you, surely they'll wait. A few weeks, you said? They'd have to wait that long if they hired someone who had to give notice before leaving a job."

"The museum would wait," Amy mused. "And probably the college, too. But the magazine... I don't think the editor of *Connoisseur's Choice* will have much patience, and I can't blame him. He needs a replacement for his roving expert before long."

Beth shot her a shrewd look. "So you *have* made up your mind which job you want."

Amy frowned. "I guess I have," she said slowly. "I didn't even know that I was leaning in that direction, until it was snatched away from me."

"So you're going to come back?"

"Do I have a choice? He's still my father." There was no need to go into the rest of it, she thought. The Sherwoods' divorce settlement was not the world's business.

"Talk to the people at the magazine. You might be surprised." Beth sealed the box with tape and set it aside. "Or maybe there's another way. Something you haven't thought of yet."

"Like turning myself into twins?" Amy said.

She went on up to the sixth floor, to the corner occupied by the executive offices. The lights were on, but the rooms seemed to be empty. Her father's personal assistant was nowhere to be seen. Amy hesitated outside the half-open door of Gavin Sherwood's corner office, remembering what had happened the last time she had come into this room. Her father, with Honey... The scene had scorched itself into her mind, and it still had the power to make her face burn with anger and embarrassment.

Don't dwell on it, she told herself. *It'll only make the job harder.* She gave the door a push and went inside. Two feet into the room, she stopped dead.

Behind her father's enormous desk sat a man, dark head bent over an open drawer. Even half-hidden as he was by the desk, there was no mistaking the power and fitness of that lean frame. He looked up almost casually as she came in, but as his gaze fell on Amy, she thought she saw his body tighten, as if every muscle was coiling, ready for action.

Was he surprised to see her, then? If he hadn't been warned, he must be even more startled at her sudden appearance than Robert and Beth had been. After all, neither Robert nor Beth had actually been a witness to that climactic confrontation between Amy and her father, while Dylan Copeland had.

Or perhaps he wasn't surprised that she'd turned up, but he was bracing himself for what she might do.

Dylan stood up slowly, with a grace which looked effortless. He was tall and broad-shouldered, but the fact that he'd discarded his jacket and rolled up the sleeves of his white shirt emphasized his powerful build and made her feel very fragile. Or was that just her imagination at work?

Not that she was fantasizing about Dylan Copeland's body, Amy told herself tartly. Any inclination she might ever have had in that direction had dissipated within a week of his coming to work for Gavin—when it became apparent that Amy amused rather than intrigued him. It was just the uncomfortable position she'd suddenly found herself in that was making her feel so brittle, not some overwhelming masculine appeal of Dylan's.

"Good morning, Amy," he said mildly. "It's a surprise to see you here. Last time you set foot in this office, you told your father you wouldn't be back until hell froze over."

"Is that what I said? I didn't remember, exactly."

"Not a very original expression, I must say. I was disappointed in you, because even under those circumstances I expected you to come up with something much more striking. But it seemed to make your point adequately."

"And of course you were listening to every word."

"I could hardly help it," Dylan pointed out. "People in west Texas might have had to strain to hear you, but for anyone who was closer than that it was no effort at all. Have a seat and tell me why you've come back." He sat down again.

"You weren't expecting me?" Amy walked across the room and perched on the corner of the desk closest to him, pushing aside a pre-Columbian statuette that her father used as a paperweight. She'd chosen the position very carefully, so she could look down at him. "I thought perhaps Gavin had phoned to warn you I was on my way, and you'd come in to clear out the personal things that you'd already moved into his desk."

"I see you still have an imagination. What a nice picture you've created of me—the moment I heard your father was tethered to a heart monitor, I made a slick play for his job." He leaned back in Gavin Sherwood's chair, appearing completely at ease.

"You're twisting my words. That's not what I meant."

"Wasn't it?" he said dryly. "So you're here to take over. And whose idea was that, I wonder. Hasn't the job hunt been successful?"

He's just trying to needle you, Amy told herself. *And he's succeeding.* "Are you volunteering to advise me about which offer I should accept? Because if that's the case, I should warn you—"

"That you'd rather flip a coin, I suppose."

"Coins don't have enough sides."

His dark eyebrows arched. "More than two? You *are* in demand, I see."

Amy held up a finger. "One, the art museum is considering me for a position as assistant curator in the textiles division."

"Only an assistant?" Dylan murmured. "I'm disappointed."

Amy ignored him and put up a second finger. "Two, I'll probably be asked to join the art faculty at the college."

"You should hold out for the dean's job."

She waggled her hand at him, three fingers extended. "And third, I could be the new roving expert for *Connoisseur's Choice.*"

"A stuffy old magazine about antiques and collectibles." Dylan shrugged. "No wonder you're coming back here instead."

"Look," Amy said. "It's already apparent that

you've got a chip on your shoulder about me being here. So let's get one thing straight. It wasn't my idea to come back, because I don't want this job. As far as I'm concerned, Gavin should have turned the whole works over to you till he's back on his feet. You've been his personal assistant for six months now, and if you can't run this business on your own for a while he ought to fire you."

"Thank you," Dylan said.

His tone was meek, but Amy saw a glint in his eyes that she thought must have been anger. But why should she be surprised? Of course he was irritated that Gavin had preferred to trust her—despite her long absence from the business—instead of him. And since Gavin wasn't around, of course Dylan was taking that irritation out on her.

"At least," he went on, "I think there may have been a compliment buried somewhere underneath all that."

Amy wasn't listening. She had suddenly remembered what Beth had said—*Maybe there's another way.*

And maybe she didn't have to turn herself into twins in order to have it all.

"I've got a proposition for you," she said suddenly.

Dylan looked around the room. "Perhaps there's something in the ventilating system," he mused. "Because propositions seem to be part of the atmosphere in this office."

Amy willed herself not to turn pink. "I'm certainly not talking about Honey's kind of proposition. Gavin's got a fixation that I'm the only one who can run this place, which is absurd."

Dylan didn't speak, but she thought she saw a gleam of agreement in his eyes.

"But frankly, I have a lot of things I'd rather do. So

let's make a deal. I'll be enough of a figurehead to keep Gavin happy, but you'll be the boss in everything but name. You can run the place as you see fit, I'll go take on my new job, and we'll both have what we want.''

Dylan was shaking his head.

"Why not?'' Amy asked crossly. "If you're holding out for the title of acting CEO, believe me, I'd give it to you if I could.''

"Titles never appealed to me much. And I'm not fond of being a sacrificial lamb, either.''

Amy gasped. "What on earth—''

"This plan of yours is a pretty nice setup—for you, that is. If I pull it off, you get the credit. But if I don't, you can tearfully confess to your father that it wasn't your fault because I was really the one at the helm all along.''

"He'd be furious at me for ignoring his wishes and putting you in charge.''

"Not as angry as he'd be if you screwed things up personally. No, Ms. Sherwood, you're not dumping this one on me. Because if you try, I'll hand you my keys— and quit.'' He rocked a little farther back in the chair. "So what are we going to do about it?''

CHAPTER TWO

AMY felt as if he'd picked up the pre-Columbian statuette from her father's desk and hit her over the head with it.

She stared at Dylan, unwilling to believe she'd heard him correctly. But his voice had been firm and absolutely level. He meant exactly what he'd said...or else he was the best poker player Amy had ever run into.

What would happen if she called his bluff? Or at least let him know that she wasn't entirely convinced he was willing to burn his bridges so completely?

She smiled. "You won't quit."

His eyes narrowed, but his tone was cordial. "If you think I'm joking, try me."

"I don't believe you'd desert my father while he's ill—and if you quit on me, it's just the same as abandoning him."

Dylan looked at her with a gleam of admiration in his dark-blue eyes. "You're almost as good a manipulator as Gavin is, you know."

"Besides, you can't just walk away from this job. Okay, maybe you're not charmed by the terms I'm talking about, but that's perfectly understandable. I'm not delighted with them, either. But—"

"Get one thing through your head, dear. I don't want your father's job any more than you do."

Doubt crept into Amy's mind. "Don't call me *dear*," she said automatically.

"Why shouldn't I? If we're not going to be working together—"

"But you'd be crazy to quit now. You've put six months into this job, and by now you must be thinking of how you'd run the business if it was left in your hands. Any red-blooded male would. And this is your opportunity to prove yourself."

Dylan shrugged. "I don't happen to have anything to prove."

"But you *can't* quit."

"Of course I can. Your father hired me, Amy. He didn't purchase me."

Amy's doubts were rapidly being overwhelmed by panic. Even though she'd suggested to Gavin that he could rely completely on his assistant, she hadn't realized how much she herself had depended on Dylan to be there as a sort of safety net. Even before she'd had the brainstorm of letting him take over entirely, she'd counted on him to lend her a hand, to bring her up to speed after her long absence.

It was bad enough that she was having to take over for her father at all. But it had never occurred to her that she might have to do it entirely by herself.

She'd been prepared for Dylan to resent her being boosted above him on the management ladder. She'd have bet her next paycheck—wherever it might come from—that he was too competitive not to object when he was passed over, especially in favor of a woman who had been gone so long she might as well be an outsider. But even then it had never occurred to her that he might actually quit.

"It never crossed my mind," she said almost to herself, "that you might not even be ambitious enough to want Gavin's job."

Only when she saw his eyes grow chilly did she realize that it might not have been a wise thing to say. Come to that, she reflected, she didn't entirely believe it even now.

But whatever his reasons were, they didn't matter at the moment—because she simply couldn't let him leave. At the same time, she could hardly let him see how desperate she was to have him stay, or he'd be waving a resignation letter at her any time things didn't go his way.

"What on earth would you do instead?" she asked. "If you quit?"

His eyebrows rose. "I do have a few talents."

"Of course," she said hastily. "But—"

"And surely, after your dramatic exit, you're in no position to tell me that it's necessary to have a second job lined up before quitting the first one."

Amy bit her lip. "No, but—"

"Especially when the boss has provoked the resignation."

"I'm trying *not* to provoke you!"

"Really? I'm afraid I missed that part. And though it's kind of you to worry about how I'll make a living, Amy, it isn't necessary. You just gave me three good leads. The college, the museum... Now what was the third one? Oh, yes, the magazine about antiques. Roving expert, hmm? That would look nice on my business card."

"If you think six months in this business makes you an expert—" She saw his eyes turn to ice once more and stopped in midsentence. True as the comment had been, why take the chance of aggravating him even more? "You can't just walk out of here, you know."

"If your next move is to tell me that I have to give

you a month's notice, you can hardly hold me to a higher standard than you used for yourself.'' He glanced at his wristwatch. ''What's it going to be, Amy?''

''What's your hurry?'' she asked irritably. ''What difference does it make to you if I take a while to think about it?'' Even though there was really nothing to think about—and it was apparent that Dylan knew it, too.

''Because if I'm going to be free for lunch, I still have time to make a date. So stop dithering and decide.''

Amy sighed and slid off the desk. ''Get out of my chair,'' she said. ''I've got work to do.''

Dylan noted with interest that she'd landed with her neat little Italian sandals placed squarely between his outstretched feet, so close that it would be nearly impossible for him to stand up without brushing against her. He considered for a moment whether she could actually have intended to issue an invitation, and concluded that she'd been too annoyed even to think about where she was standing.

Just as well, he thought. The last thing he needed was to get tangled up with his new boss, and he'd better remember it. She'd already made a few uncomfortably shrewd comments. Accidentally, he was sure, but if he'd had any idea just how astute Amy Sherwood could be without even trying, he wouldn't have left the decision of whether he stayed or left in her hands.

But he had offered her the choice, and he couldn't back out now without causing the very curiosity he was trying to avoid. So the key was to keep her too busy to think. Too busy to ask questions.

''What's first?'' he asked as he stood up.

Amy turned at the same moment, and his cheek brushed against the dark brown cloud of hair. Obviously, he thought with a flicker of regret, he'd read her correctly, for she leaped back, bumping into the corner of the desk and almost staggering.

He put a hand on her shoulder to keep her from losing her balance. Yes, her hair was as soft as that fleeting touch had suggested. It lay like silk over his fingers.

"What do you think you're doing?" she snapped, shrugging his hand away.

"Following orders," Dylan said innocently. "You told me to get out of your chair."

"I didn't tell you to hug me." She sat down with a thump.

"If that's what you call a hug, it's no wonder you…" He saw the gold sparks of anger in her eyes and prudently moved around the desk to a safer distance. "Which stack of folders do you want first? Do you want to bring yourself up to date on the auctions that are coming up next, or start with the list of people Gavin was cultivating?"

She looked thoughtful. "You've talked to the people he's been working with, haven't you?"

"Most of them, I suppose."

"Then you can tell me much more about them than a bunch of dry notes can."

She looked very small and fragile, sitting in Gavin's too-big chair. Dylan told himself this was no time to get a Galahad complex. In fact, his best move would be to keep all the distance possible between him and Amy Sherwood.

But the message didn't seem to get through from his brain to his tongue. "I'll get the folders," he heard himself say, "and we can go through them together."

The once-neat surface of Gavin Sherwood's desk looked like a filing cabinet had exploded on it. Untidy stacks of file folders nearly covered the polished teak. Those detailing Gavin's dealings with prospective clients were piled on the southeast corner, while upcoming auctions occupied the southwest corner. Amy's head was bent over her father's desk calendar when Dylan pushed the door open and came in, carrying a large white paper bag.

"Don't you believe in knocking?" she asked absent-mindedly. "I hope you can read the cryptic codes Gavin uses to keep his schedule straight, because I certainly can't. He's got something written on the page for today, but it could be either 'confer with Rex' or 'confirm tickets.' Or maybe it's 'conifer forest.'"

Dylan grinned. "As far as I know, he hasn't taken up tree-hugging. If it's for this evening, I expect he meant Rex Maxwell."

Amy reached for a folder in the pile of prospective clients. "The one who's thinking of selling his Picasso?"

"That's the one." He started to unload small waxed paper boxes from the bag.

Amy pushed the folder aside to make room. "How much do I owe you for lunch?"

"Nothing, but next time it's your turn to buy."

Amy glanced at the files stacked on the desk. At this rate, there were going to be plenty of "next times." She hadn't even made a dent in the piles.

"The Maxwells are having a cocktail party tonight," Dylan went on. "The invitation is on my desk because I was just about to phone them with Gavin's regrets when you came in."

"You might let them know I'll be coming instead."

"*I* might let them know?" Dylan tipped his head to one side. "This," he said, pointing to the telephone on her desk, "is an instrument of communication. Do you know why it's here? Because you pick it up and press the buttons and talk to the person who answers."

Amy stared at him in disbelief. "What difference does it make if you call the Maxwells about Gavin or about me?"

"You're not confined to a hospital bed."

"You mean you don't make calls for Gavin when he's here? What kind of personal assistant refuses to use the telephone?"

"One who is not a secretary." He handed her a pair of chopsticks.

How ridiculous could he be? "You didn't object to going downstairs to wait for the deliveryman. That's pretty secretarial."

"Oh, but that's different."

"Why? Because you were hungry?"

"You got it in one try. Congratulations. Anyway, it'll be your turn tomorrow."

Amy dipped her chopsticks into a container of sweet and sour chicken. "Take a letter, Mr. Copeland. To whom it may concern—that's you, of course. This is to inform you that there has been a change in policy concerning the duties of personal assistant—that's also you—to the acting CEO—that's me—"

Dylan was still wielding his chopsticks. "Sorry, boss. I don't do dictation, either. If you'd like to get someone up here from the secretarial pool, call extension seventy-two."

Amy fixed him with a look. "And how would you know that, if Gavin does all his own telephoning?"

"Because whenever I need typing or photocopies, I call them."

Of course. "It's a shame you don't do shorthand. It

wouldn't be nearly as fun dictating a character reference for you if you're not enjoying every word along with me." She set the chicken aside and investigated a container that seemed to hold mostly broccoli. "Gavin made a note on tomorrow's schedule, too. It's something about running an errand, I think, but I don't have any idea what."

Dylan glanced at the calendar. "Not running an errand. Just running."

"You mean like jogging? My father doesn't jog."

"Maybe he didn't in his previous life."

Another thing we have to thank Honey for, Amy thought. *I wonder if that's why he had the heart attack.* She kept her voice level. "How often does he do this?"

"Whenever he thinks it's time to once again nudge Mitchell Harlow into thinking about getting rid of his family's autograph collection."

"I should have known it wasn't for the exercise," Amy said glumly.

"Mitchell runs through Country Club Plaza every Tuesday, Thursday and Saturday morning starting at 6:00 a.m. sharp. Rain or shine, he's religious about it— and it's the only time you can rely on catching him. So about once a week Gavin's been going, too."

"And this collection of autographs is worth it?"

"Gavin hasn't actually seen it, but someone who has told him it includes Martin Luther and Catherine the Great."

Amy sighed. "Then I guess I'm going jogging in the morning."

"Your father would be proud of you."

His face was perfectly straight, but Amy was certain she detected a note of suppressed laughter in Dylan's voice. What she wouldn't give to make him swallow his amusement...but once she started to think about ways to get even, the answer was obvious. "Of course, I wouldn't know Mitchell Harlow if I tripped over him, so I'll need you to come along and introduce me. Six in the morning, you said? Shall I pick you up?" She was pleased to see that his face had tightened just a little.

Dylan began gathering up the debris of their lunch. "No, thanks. I'll meet you at the fountain."

"Wait a minute—the Plaza has at least a hundred fountains."

"The big one. Neptune and the seahorses. I'll get you the Maxwells' invitation so you can let them know you're coming."

Amy bit her lip to keep from smiling at the resigned note in his voice. *That evens things up a little,* she thought. *And about time, too.*

It took Amy all afternoon to make a perceptible dent in the stacks of files Dylan had sorted out for her to look at, and the experience had left her with a new appreciation of the challenges of her father's job. Then, just as she was congratulating herself for everything she'd accomplished, Dylan appeared with yet another stack.

Amy wanted to groan. "What are those?"

"More prospects that I found lurking on top of a filing cabinet. Gavin must have left them there instead of putting them back."

"Let me guess. You don't file, either."

"Of course I file, but only the things I pull out myself."

"Good. You'll know right where to put all these back when I'm finished with them."

He didn't comment, but Amy had the feeling he'd like

to. Instead, he said, "Perhaps I should warn you that the Maxwells are sticklers for punctuality."

"I'm on my way right now." She dug her handbag from the bottom drawer.

"I'll leave these here on the desk so they'll be ready when you come in tomorrow."

"Don't turn the lights out when you leave," Amy ordered, "just in case those folders act like coat hangers and multiply in the dark."

Downstairs, the sales room was still quiet, with no auction scheduled until the weekend. But under the watchful eye of the sales staff, a half-dozen people were studying the furniture displayed in the showrooms, browsing through the catalog and even measuring the pieces.

The waiting room was half-full of people waiting their turn to inspect the merchandise, and at the desk Robert was looking harried. He paused as Amy passed the desk, however, and called her name. When she turned, he stretched out a hand to her.

"I didn't know when you came in this morning that you were staying, Ms. Sherwood," he said. "Things have been a little uncertain around here for the past few days, with your father so sick. But now—well, the whole staff is thanking heaven that you're back where you belong."

Amy could have sworn his eyes were misty. "I'll try not to destroy your faith in me," she said, keeping her voice as light as she could.

She rushed home to change her clothes and found the red light blinking madly on her answering machine. Remembering how the simple act of picking up her messages that morning had fractured her life, she almost ignored this batch. But habit made her push the button anyway, turning the volume up so she could listen from her bedroom while she changed.

Her mother had called. Just to chat, she'd said, and to invite Amy to stop in over the weekend and see her new furniture. She sounded almost normal, Amy thought. Only someone who knew her very well would have detected strain in Carol's voice.

The second call was from the head curator of the museum. She swore under her breath. Dylan had kept her so buried in files that she'd completely forgotten to make the necessary calls to warn her prospective employers of the sudden hitch in her plans.

Funny, she thought, how it had taken that speed bump to help her see what it was she really wanted to do. She didn't mind calling the museum and the college to let them know that she wouldn't be available after all. But the magazine…the magazine was a little different.

Connoisseur's Choice was far from being the stuffy old publication that Dylan had suggested it was. It was a glossy, sophisticated monthly magazine which covered an enormous range of both genuine antiques and interesting collectibles. A sort of reference book which happened to be published in segments, the magazine had actually become a collectible itself, for there was a brisk demand for secondhand issues—even ten-year-old ones. If in doubt, buyers and collectors consulted *Connoisseur's Choice,* and they ignored its suggestions at their peril. Just to be associated with the magazine was to become an instant authority.

As for the position of roving expert, it might have been fashioned especially for Amy. "We're looking for someone who has experience with everything," the editor had told her. "Not just priceless paintings or handhammered silver or Tang horses. Our readers are interested in those things, certainly, but not many of them will ever own one. We need someone who's interested in, and knowledgeable about, things like political buttons and movie posters and patent medicine bottles.''

"Someone exactly like me, Brad," Amy had said. And though Brad Parker hadn't committed himself at the time, he had seemed to agree.

Earlier in the week, he had called to tell her that the publisher liked her credentials and he expected to be able to make her an offer within a few days. And now she was going to have to tell him that she wouldn't be able to take the job for a month at least—and hope that he wanted her badly enough to wait.

It was a rotten shame, she thought, that Dylan Copeland hadn't jumped at the chance to prove himself by taking over the helm at Sherwood Auctions. Odd, too. The one thing she would never have suspected of him was a shortage of initiative.

She hailed a cab to take her to the Maxwells' apartment tower rather than risk finding a place to park, because she'd cut things a little finer than she'd planned. She was still trying to catch her breath as she rang the Maxwells' doorbell on the top floor just a couple of minutes after the hour specified on the invitation.

A bluff, hearty man greeted her, and Amy apologized for being late. "I'm afraid I didn't allow time for a security check, but the guard downstairs was quite troubled over the fact that I don't look like a *Mr.* Sherwood."

Rex Maxwell laughed heartily. "I'm glad to know Pete doesn't need his eyes examined," he said and guided her over to the bar. Immediately the doorbell chimed again and he moved off to answer it.

Just as well, Amy thought. She could hardly ask him straight off whether he'd decided to auction the Picasso.

With a glass in her hand, she began to wander through the apartment. The rooms were huge and bare-looking, with blocky steel furniture and the occasional modern painting on the walls. She saw nothing of the caliber of a Picasso, though. Did they keep it in a vault somewhere? If so, she understood why they were thinking of selling it, because there was little point in owning a painting like that if you couldn't see and enjoy it.

Or had the painting already gone to some other auction house?

Until now, her feelings about Gavin's fears of losing his clients had been almost academic, but suddenly the threat had become much more personal. She felt her chest tightening.

Remember the size of that stack of files, she reminded herself. Her father must have been working on a hundred prospective clients. Some of them simply had to come through; the percentages were in her favor.

Still, the sheer size of the number was not as reassuring as Amy would have liked it to be. If—despite all his experience and contacts—Gavin needed to work on a hundred prospects in order to end up with just a few auctions, then how could she hope to snare enough business to satisfy his needs?

She saw a familiar face here and there in the crowd, mostly people that she'd happened to notice when they had attended auctions but a few that she'd worked with directly in the last couple of years.

One of them, a blue-haired matron, came up to her. "How's your mother doing these days, Amy?"

Amy flinched. Why, she wondered, did people insist on asking her about Carol's health and Gavin's marital plans? Because they felt uncomfortable calling up Carol or Gavin, she supposed. But did they honestly expect Amy to spill the gory details?

"I haven't talked to her for a few days," she said honestly.

The woman sniffed. "I suppose that shouldn't be a surprise, now that you've taken sides with your father."

Unbelieving, Amy stared at her. "What on earth makes you think that?"

"My friend called me a few minutes ago. Cell phones are wonderful things, aren't they?" She patted her handbag. "Our whole bridge club has them now. She was in the waiting room at Sherwood Auctions a few minutes ago and heard that you've started working there again."

"News certainly travels quickly," Amy said.

"And what does Carol think of you making up with your father?"

If she knew the whole story she'd probably be thrilled. "Why don't you ask her?" Amy said coolly. "I'm sure she'd love to hear from her friends."

The matron fixed her with a stare. "I don't know what your father is thinking of, the old goat," she said. "Taking up with a bimbo, at his age. No wonder his heart attacked him."

She's just fishing, Amy told herself. *Trying to get a reaction.* "Shall I tell him you're devastated that another obligation will prevent you from attending his wedding?" she asked gently. "Excuse me, I see someone I must speak with."

She moved through the crowd, nodding and smiling at people she didn't even see, still shaken by the encounter.

She'd known, of course, that the Sherwoods' friends would be startled by the divorce and stunned by Gavin's choice of a new wife. And not only their friends objected, either—on the night of his heart attack, Amy had heard one of Gavin's nurses mutter something about Honey being so dim she couldn't spell CPR. But it hadn't occurred to Amy that so many people would take the matter personally, much less feel they had a right to comment.

That very direct animosity wasn't going to make her job any easier, Amy reflected. It wasn't only Gavin's heart attack that had threatened his business.

She reached the far end of the room and turned back, and her gaze snagged on the Picasso. It was hanging alone on a stark white wall, and nearby stood a woman who looked as much like the figure in the painting as it was possible for a living human to resemble the modernistic form. Her face was all sharp angles and shadows, and the individual features—though not unpleasing—didn't seem to belong together. As Amy watched, the woman waved a hand casually toward the painting and spoke animatedly to the man standing next to her.

Amy studied the man and, recognizing him, allowed herself to breathe again. He was a bright light of local industry, not an appraiser or art expert or auctioneer, as she'd feared. For the moment at least, the Picasso was still within her reach.

"It's a very nice painting," said a man standing next to her. "But you shouldn't look at it with that covetous expression, Amy. Mrs. Maxwell might object."

Amy looked up at the editor of *Connoisseur's Choice.* "Hi, Brad," she said, trying not to sound breathless. "I didn't expect to see you here."

"Oh, we get invited to all the best parties. It's one of the perks of working for the magazine."

"Speaking of the magazine," Amy began, "I was going to call you tomorrow."

"Getting anxious? It does seem to have taken the publisher forever to make up his mind. But he finally gave me the go-ahead this afternoon to offer you the job at the salary we discussed. When can you start?"

"That's the problem, I'm afraid. Until my father's back on his feet…"

She tried to explain why she was needed so badly at Sherwood Auctions for a while, but the hollow feeling inside her expanded as she watched Brad's face darken.

"I was hoping to have a new roving expert on board next week," he said. "Waiting a month or more…I don't know what the publisher's going to say, Amy."

"He's the one who's taken three weeks to make up his mind that he wanted me at all," she argued.

"As far as that goes, Mr. Dougal's getting old and a bit unpredictable these days. We've learned not to expect him to make snap decisions. But when he does make up his mind—"

"But what's the difference if it's a little longer before I can start? Almost everyone you hire must have some loose ends to tie up before they can start work."

Brad swirled the ice cubes which were all that remained of his drink. "I'll have to run it past him again and let you know." He turned toward the bar.

"Good," Amy called after him. "By the time he gets back to you, I'll be free. In the meantime, you can find me at Sherwood Auctions—working hard so I can get out of there in a hurry."

With a sigh, she set her own glass on the tray of a passing waiter. The party was already starting to break up, she realized. The Maxwells, it seemed, not only expected their guests to arrive punctually but to depart the same way.

Amy hung back till the crowd thinned, hoping for a

chance to have a private word with her hosts. If they *were* thinking of selling the Picasso...

Now that she'd seen it, she had no doubt of the painting's value. It was a major work which would bring millions at auction, and the commission for Sherwood Auctions would be a significant chunk of cash.

She multiplied the figures in her head and concluded that this one deal could produce enough money to solve Gavin's financial crunch in one blow. She wouldn't even have to wait for the auction to actually be held. As soon as the Maxwells had signed an agreement, Amy could turn all the arrangements over to Dylan and go off to *Connoisseur's Choice* with a clear conscience. She'd be happy and Gavin would be ecstatic. Dylan might not be thrilled, but he was certainly capable of carrying out the details.

If only she could pull it off.

Eventually there was a moment when the Maxwells were standing alone by the front door, and Amy seized her chance. "Thank you for letting me come in my father's place tonight." She held out her business card. It was part of the outdated supply that she should have thrown away after she resigned from the auction house. It still listed her as an appraiser—but at least the Maxwells would have her name right. "Gavin will be back to work in a few weeks, but he's asked me to tell you that if you make a decision about the Picasso in the meantime he's authorized me to act for him in arranging the sale."

Mrs. Maxwell stared at the business card she was holding as if it had abruptly turned into a cockroach. She suddenly looked even more like the impossible woman of the painting, and her voice had turned to ice. "What are you talking about?"

Rex Maxwell shifted from one foot to the other. "Now, my dear…a mistake…anyone could misunderstand… Gavin must have thought…"

His wife turned on him. "You talked to Gavin Sherwood about selling my Picasso?" The accusation cut sharply across the remaining party conversation.

Rex Maxwell glared at Amy, but his voice was mild, almost pacifying. "The possibility came up," he admitted. "I didn't say yes or no."

He was lying, and Amy knew it. The glare he'd sent her way told her that he and Gavin *had* seriously discussed the sale—but Rex Maxwell had never consulted his wife about it.

She felt unsteady on her feet, as if the apartment tower had suddenly begun swaying in a high wind.

Now it made sense that Gavin's note had mentioned only the husband. The only remaining question was whether he had known his friend was working behind his wife's back. Had he even suspected it, or had he been as innocent as Amy herself?

Not that it mattered now what Gavin might have known, because the cat was most definitely out of the bag.

It was too bad the apartment tower was entirely air-conditioned and the windows were all the tightly sealed sort, Amy thought. Because right now would be a perfect time to throw herself out of one.

CHAPTER THREE

MUCH to Dylan's surprise, Amy was already waiting for him when he walked up to the Neptune fountain, at the corner of the Plaza shopping district, at precisely six o'clock the next morning. She was sitting on a bench with her head in her hands, and she didn't look up as he approached. In fact, she didn't even flinch when his Irish setter plopped at her feet, panting from the run they'd already had, with her tail slapping against Amy's ankles.

"You'd better stay a little more alert to your surroundings," he suggested. "A mugger who saw you sitting there that way would think you're a pretty tasty morsel."

"Who cares?" Her voice was muffled by her palms. "Bring on the muggers."

Dylan wrapped the dog's leash around his wrist and put one foot up on the bench, stretching his muscles to keep them limber in the still-cool air of a mid-May morning. He didn't look at her, and he kept his voice carefully neutral. "It must have been quite a cocktail party last night if it left you with a hangover of those proportions."

She looked up at him with her small, pointed chin aggressively thrust out. "It wasn't how much I drank that was the problem."

"I suppose you're claiming it was food poisoning instead," he scoffed. "They all say that."

"No, I didn't get a funny-tasting sausage." She

sighed. "The problem is…well, I didn't just put my foot in my mouth. I shoved it so far down my throat that a surgeon could remove my appendix and trim my toenails all in the same operation."

Dylan stopped stretching and looked at her more closely. "That bad, huh? Who'd you insult?"

"The Maxwells, of course. I committed a major *faux pax*, and even though I apologized all over myself, I barely made it out alive." She fixed her gaze on him. "If I thought for an instant that you knew Rex Maxwell was trying to sell that Picasso behind his wife's back, and you didn't warn me, I'd… I'd…"

She apparently couldn't conjure up a punishment that was bad enough. Dylan decided not to give her a chance to think about it. "No, I didn't set you up," he said. "But now you see why I didn't want to be the one in charge."

"Thank you very much for the sympathy."

"At least you're efficient. Your methods leave no question that any more time spent on the Picasso would be wasted."

She gave a little moan.

"I wonder why he wanted to put it up for auction in the first place," Dylan mused, "if he knew his wife was likely to object."

"He said Gavin misunderstood him and he never had any intention of selling."

Dylan considered and shook his head. "You know better than to think Gavin makes that sort of mistake. More likely Rex Maxwell is in financial difficulties and doesn't want to confess to the wife. Not that it matters to us. Scratch the Picasso and move on to the next possibility." He felt a shudder run through her. "What's the matter? From the sound of things, it can't get worse than that experience.''

''I certainly hope not,'' she said drearily. ''Where's a good, efficient mugger when you need one? If somebody hit me over the head, maybe I'd lose my memory along with my wallet.''

''Put the whole thing behind you.'' He held out a hand to pull her up. ''Come on. A couple of miles through the Plaza and you'll be a new woman.'' He stepped back to look at her appraisingly. ''Nice shorts. Not only are they attention-seeking pink, but they fit just right.''

''Don't flatter yourself that I'm out to impress you. This was the only pair I could lay hands on this morning in the dark.''

''I know perfectly well you're not trying to impress me,'' he said gently. ''You were just trying to attract muggers.''

She began to stretch. The dog, who knew the routine, stood up and whined, eager to be off again, and for the first time Amy seemed to notice her. ''Aren't you a beauty?''

The setter tossed her head bashfully and sneezed.

''And she's modest, too,'' Dylan said. ''Give her a compliment and she promptly proves that she's only human. Or something like that.''

''How far have you run already?''

''A mile or so. Reggie would rather run in Loose Park, but she'll make do with the Plaza if she has to.''

''Well, I don't imagine she gets the same excitement from window-shopping that people do.'' Amy dropped into step beside him, and Reggie loped easily ahead. ''Do you live somewhere around here? If you usually run in Loose Park—that's the one just south of the Plaza, isn't it?''

Around the corner ahead of them, Dylan spotted a jogger turning into their path and interrupted her. "There's Mitchell Harlow, right on time." He lengthened his stride in order to catch up, and glanced over his shoulder to see if Amy was having trouble keeping the pace.

Her gaze was fixed on their quarry, and she looked startled. Dylan realized that from his description of Mitchell Harlow's jogging routine, she'd probably expected an athlete instead of a short, prematurely balding, not-quite-rotund man in a purple running suit.

Amy speeded up till she was beside him again. "He doesn't have a wife who'll have a fit about selling his autograph collection, does he?"

"The last I heard, he wasn't married."

"And exactly how long has that been? Last week? A year?"

Dylan grinned at her and raised his voice. "Good morning, Mitchell."

Mitchell Harlow turned his head to return the greeting, but he saw Amy first and the words seemed to stick in his throat.

It was the sort of reaction Dylan had expected—especially after he'd noticed the pink shorts himself. So he certainly had no reason to feel irritated by the bug-eyed way Mitchell Harlow was goggling at Amy.

It was obvious that Amy had also noted the interest in Mitchell Harlow's eyes, for there was a gleam in her own. Dylan wondered if she was speculating whether in this case, unlike with the Maxwells, she had an advantage that her father didn't.

Though Mitchell had been awestruck by Amy's appearance, he found his voice quickly enough when Dylan introduced her. "Sherwood?" he said. "Are you related to the guy who's always nagging me to sell my autograph collection?''

She shot a look at Dylan, who shrugged. He'd done his best; now it was up to her.

''I heard somewhere he'd taken up with quite a dish,'' Mitchell went on. ''But I had no idea what kind of dish we were talking about.''

Dylan glanced sideways at Amy, curious to see how she would react to being confused with Honey. She looked a little like a firecracker just before the explosion—sparks and all. He stepped nimbly into the breach. ''That's a different dish, Mitchell. This one's his daughter.''

Amy glared at him as if to say that she was perfectly capable of handling Mitchell Harlow by herself. *Fine,* Dylan thought, and he allowed Reggie to pull him a few paces ahead of the other two. But he could still hear most of the conversation.

''I understand your autograph collection is pretty special,'' Amy said. ''You must spend a lot of time with it.''

''Haven't looked at it in six months, I suppose,'' Mitchell panted. ''But I know why your old man is so anxious to get his hands on it. He thinks he can make a pretty penny.''

''No doubt he does.'' Amy's voice was cool. ''We're not in business for the fun of it. Of course, if Sherwood Auctions stands to make a nice chunk on the commission, that means you'd make a whole lot more.''

''Now don't you start on me,'' Mitchell complained.

''Why should I care what you do? It's none of my business if you choose to keep money tied up in autographs you never look at when you could spend it for something you'd really enjoy. A Lamborghini, maybe, or a yacht. Nice to meet you, Mr. Harlow." She raised her voice. "Isn't this where we turn off, Dylan?"

Back at the Neptune fountain, she sank onto the bench to regain her breath. Dylan surveyed her with interest. "That was a neat move, right up to the point where you broke away. You might have gotten somewhere with him if you'd pushed just a little harder—and not told him he was being a fool to hang onto something he doesn't even like."

"And maybe if I kept on I'd have just annoyed him," Amy said. "If Gavin hasn't gotten anywhere by talking to him, why should I expect anything different? Besides, that stack of folders is too high for me to waste my time on reluctant clients—to say nothing of the fact that my legs were giving out on me. I'm a walker, not a jogger."

Curiosity nagged at him. "Why is this all so important to you? Your father's been working on Mitchell Harlow and the Picasso and that whole list of other people for months, but you're going after them as if you only have this week."

"Isn't building up business always important?" But she didn't meet his eyes. "Want a ride home? My car's parked over there."

"No, thanks," he said. "Reggie and I'll run."

She bent to retrieve a key that had been fastened to her shoestring, retied her shoe, and stood up. "See you at the office in a little while then."

Reggie was impatient to be off, but Dylan ignored the dog's tug on her leash and watched the enticing sway of Amy's hips as she crossed the street to her car. However, it wasn't entirely the attention-seizing pink shorts that occupied his mind.

Why was she trying so very hard to prove herself?

*   *   *

The coffee in the employees' lounge was industrial strength—Amy made a mental note that if she ever needed to take the varnish off a piece of furniture, it would probably work as well as commercial strippers. But she poured herself a cup anyway and carried it up to Gavin's office.

She surveyed the stacks of folders, thinking that somehow there didn't seem to be as many of them as there had been yesterday. But she knew the stacks were actually just as high; it was her attitude which had changed. This morning, Gavin's list of potential clients no longer looked nearly as promising.

In little more than twelve hours, she'd killed one potential auction and crossed another one off Gavin's short list. So much for her plan to nail one big deal and get out. At this rate, within a week she'd be out all right— but only because there were no more potential clients to approach.

She knew Dylan was right about the Picasso. Since it was too late to mend the error, there was no sense in wasting regret on the situation. And she knew she'd been right about Mitchell Harlow—if he considered Gavin's occasional mention of the autographs to be nagging, then more of the same wasn't likely to convince him.

The question she was asking herself now was whether the other potential clients on Gavin's list were any more promising. Had her father simply been fooling himself? Had his attention been so concentrated on Honey that he'd seen possibilities where none really existed?

It had been one thing to put aside her own plans to help her father out of a bind. But to give up her dreams and end up with zero to show for it....

Was she sacrificing a future at *Connoisseur's Choice* for nothing?

The low, repeated buzz of a telephone from the next room rasped on her nerves. It was Dylan's phone, but he wasn't there yet to answer it. "He obviously doesn't come to work on any particular schedule, either," she muttered. "I wonder what he *does* do around here." She picked up her own phone and cut in on the call. "Dylan Copeland's office. May I help you?"

A long silence greeted her, followed by the hesitant-sounding voice of a woman. "I didn't know he'd hired a secretary."

"He hasn't exactly. I'm filling in." Amy was frowning. She thought for an instant that she recognized the voice, but why would her mother be calling Dylan? *I must be wrong,* Amy decided. Maybe she'd thought the woman sounded familiar because deep down she was feeling a little guilty about not having told her mother about her change in job plans. If Carol heard about it from someone else—that old cat who'd been at the Maxwells' party last night, for instance…

"Amy?" Carol Sherwood sounded stunned. "What are you doing there?"

Amy sighed. *When I suspect I might be in trouble, why do I always have to be right?* "It's kind of a long story, Mom. Can you meet me for lunch today?"

"I've got bridge club," Carol said. "But come by the house tonight. I'll make us a salad and you can see my new furniture, too."

"I didn't know you were redecorating till you left that message last night."

There was a shrug in Carol's voice. "I didn't really plan to, but there were a few things your father wanted to take, and a few that I didn't want to have around anymore. And once I started shopping, one thing just led to another. It was time for a new look anyway. After living with antiques all these years…''

Just another bit of housecleaning, Amy thought. She couldn't blame her mother for trying to eliminate painful reminders.

The office door opened and Dylan backed in, a large foam cup in each hand. He set one on Amy's desk and started to retreat.

She shook her head and pointed to the phone, then to him. He nodded. ''I'll take it in my office.''

She interrupted her mother just as Carol began to describe the truckload of furniture which had arrived a few days ago. ''Dylan just came in. Hold on a minute.''

Amy waited until he picked up the phone with a cheery good-morning, as if he not only knew who was on the line but had expected the call. She sat staring into the distance, drinking the gourmet coffee he'd brought, until the light on the phone went out. Then she called his name.

He was carrying his coffee cup and a clipboard when he came back into her office.

''Since when have you and my mother been regular phone pals?'' Amy asked.

She'd half expected that he would deny it, or at least fidget under the question. But his voice was level. ''Since she's been calling me every day to ask about Gavin's health.''

Amy opened her mouth but no words came out. She shut it again.

''You're surprised.''

''And you're not? This has hardly been your basic amicable divorce. On the other hand, if she's been checking on him—''

''Don't get any romantic notions,'' Dylan warned.

"Being concerned about his heart isn't the same as wanting him back."

Amy thought it over. "So what you're really saying is that legally a divorce might be final in just ninety days, but emotionally it takes longer."

"Ninety days is only a beginning, I'd say. To stop caring about someone you've shared your life with—"

"Well, that makes sense." She sighed. "As for sharing a life... You know, if you'd asked me four months ago, I'd have said my parents were as happy as any couple who's been married for thirty years. I don't remember them arguing over anything."

"Sometimes that's because there's nothing left worth arguing about."

"Of course then there was the explosion over Honey, and they made up for it. Still, I don't understand why Mom's been calling you. If she wanted to know how Gavin was doing, why didn't she ask me?"

"I don't know. Perhaps she was afraid you'd think she was asking you to spy. Or maybe it's because she didn't want you to misunderstand the reason she was interested."

"Just as you thought I would," Amy said dryly. "Because kids always have this happy fantasy of their divorced parents getting back together. Well, I'm not eight years old anymore, and I'm a little more realistic than that."

"Or it could be even simpler than that. Perhaps she thought you wouldn't know, because you haven't exactly been hanging around the hospital every day, checking up on him."

"Is that where you've been this morning, and why you're late?"

"I've been stopping in every day, yes, to keep him

up to date about what's going on here, and to ask any questions that have come up.''

Amy muttered, ''Bet he got a bang out of the Picasso story.''

''I'm sure he would have, if I'd told him what happened. But since I didn't want to send his blood pressure through the roof, I thought that one could wait.''

''Too bad. Maybe he'd have fired me and my troubles would be over.'' Amy shifted a pile of folders. ''I want to order some flowers. And don't waste time telling me that you don't send flowers for the boss, because I've already figured that out. But I bet you send a few yourself, so don't expect me to believe that you don't know who the best florist is.''

He reached for the phone book. ''If you're ordering a bouquet for Mrs. Maxwell, I hope you're not considering forget-me-nots.''

She pretended not to hear him. ''It may not do any good to send her a dozen roses, but I figure the gesture can't hurt. Thanks for the coffee, by the way.''

''I thought after the run this morning you'd probably need all the help you could get to stay awake.'' He handed her the phone book, the corner of a page turned back to mark the spot. ''Did you really think I'd tell your father about the fiasco with the Maxwells?''

''Why not? It would have made you look pretty good in comparison.''

''Is that why you told me in the first place? So I'd report it to him?''

''No,'' Amy said slowly.

''You didn't have to confess what had really happened, you know. You could have just said that the Maxwells had decided not to sell after all. And it would have been the truth—even if not the entire truth.''

The fact was, Amy realized, it had never occurred to her not to tell Dylan. That was strange, she thought. She'd still been pretty much in shock, of course, even hours after the encounter with the Maxwells. But to have blurted out something which showed her in such a damaging light, to a man she hardly knew—a man who had good reason to see her as an interloper and a competitor—was hardly like her.

"I don't know why I told you," she said finally. "I guess because we're sort of stuck in this mess together."

He let the silence draw out until she finally looked up from the pencil she was fidgeting with to see that he was watching her intently. She tried to turn away from that concentrated gaze, fearful of what he might see—or think he saw—in her face. But she couldn't stop staring at him, and wondering what he saw.

"I'm glad you did," he said. His voice was low.

The telephone on her desk rang, sounding as shrill as a scream to Amy's overly keen senses. She fumbled for it and knocked it off the desk, and scrambled, red-faced, to retrieve it. What a perfectly sophomoric thing to do, she accused herself.

Robert, at the reception desk, was too well-trained to ask about all the thumps and bangs. "Ms. Sherwood, Miss Lambert is here."

For an instant, Amy actually didn't recognize the name. She frowned, and then it clicked. "You mean Honey's here? But what for?" *It can't be about Gavin,* she thought. *If he'd been worse this morning, Dylan would have told me.*

"She didn't say, Ms. Sherwood." Robert's voice was guarded.

Amy could hear the rest of the sentence as clearly as

if he'd actually said the words. *And Mr. Sherwood instructed me never to ask.*

"Sorry, Robert," she said briskly, "I forgot you can't exactly speak openly. Someone will be right down to meet her." She hung up and looked thoughtfully across at Dylan.

"Someone?" he repeated, sounding wary.

"I suppose you're going to tell me you don't act as an escort for Gavin's visitors, either?"

"No, because he thinks it's more flattering if he greets them in reception himself. Besides, Honey would be quite annoyed if she didn't command the attention of the person at the top of the pyramid."

"Well, that may have been true when it was Gavin sitting at this desk, but I hardly think she'd object to being met by a handsome young man. I'm sure she'd much rather cry on your shoulder than on mine. Figuratively speaking, of course."

Dylan's eyebrows rose slightly. "If I thought you'd actually meant that as a compliment, Amy—"

"What?" She had spoken so casually that she had to think back over what she'd said to find what he was talking about. Now why had that comment slipped out of her mouth? Not that it wasn't true, for he was handsome, but... "You're right, Dylan," she said hastily. "I didn't mean a word of it. I'm just trying to manipulate you."

A smile tugged at the corner of his mouth. "Besides, Honey's probably here to look through the showrooms. She does that now and then, and you're much better prepared to answer her questions about the merchandise than I am. You're the expert."

"You mean she's actually trying to learn about Gavin's business?" Amy said thoughtfully. "Maybe

I've underestimated the woman after all. This I have to see.''

Honey was sitting in the waiting room, slim legs crossed and toes pointed. She appeared to be inspecting one of her extraordinarily high-heeled shoes, while the middle-aged man sitting across from her seemed to be inspecting Honey. Amy didn't blame him, for Honey was quite something to look at. Her black leather skirt was slim and tight, and though her blouse was fashionably oversized, it didn't look baggy as it might have on another woman; instead it managed to hint of interesting curves underneath. As Amy came in, Honey stood up and ran an appraising eye over her. Suddenly Amy felt as if her cream-colored suit was rumpled and ill-fitting and belonged in the rag bin.

"Good morning, Honey," Amy said. "If you'd like to come with me..."

Honey stood up. The man across from her leaped to his feet as if pulled by strings. Honey gave him an abstracted half smile and allowed Amy to hold the door for her.

"How is my father feeling this morning?" Amy asked.

Honey paused. "Just fine, I'm sure. At least I haven't heard anything different."

"You haven't been to the hospital yet?"

"Sweetie, what's the point? It's all confusion in that place till noon at least. I'll stop by later, if I have time. I'm here to look through the showrooms."

"I believe we have a particularly fine collection of furniture right now."

"You believe?"

"I haven't had a chance to look at everything myself yet." And why she hadn't thought to point that fact out to Dylan.... *You're the expert,* indeed. Not in this case, when she'd never even seen the merchandise.

"I don't see why I need an escort just to look through the showrooms."

"In case you have questions," Amy said gently.

"I know what I like. What other questions are there?" Honey listened for a moment to the soft strains of a Schubert serenade on the sound system and wrinkled her nose. "I don't know why Gavin insists on that ancient music. Why not switch to something that would get people into the mood to buy things?"

"What do you have in mind?" Amy asked.

"Something that has a beat, at least. It would certainly be better than the whiny stuff." Honey bypassed the stack of catalogs by the showroom door and went inside.

Amy picked up a catalog and flipped through it. The size of a thick magazine, it listed and described each item to be sold in the upcoming auction. On the glossy cover was a photograph of the Chippendale highboy which stood just inside the showroom.

Honey was looking into the bottom drawer of the highboy. "I ask you, would you want to store your lingerie in a chest that's full of antique dust?"

"It's very expensive dust," Amy murmured.

Honey tilted her head. "How expensive?"

Amy opened the catalog, read the full description of the highboy, and made an educated guess.

Honey shook her head. "I could buy a roomful of new stuff for that much money. Besides, it gives me the creeps to think that some dead person used it before me." She closed the drawer and moved on to a mirror hanging on the wall. "Who on earth is going to buy a mirror with the silver flaking off the back? You can't see anything in it."

"Quite a number of people will be interested, considering that it happens to be very early eighteenth century, Italian, etched glass in a gilt frame. They'll make allowances for some wear, considering it's almost three hundred years old."

Honey inspected it again and shook her head. "I don't get it. The whole point of a mirror is to look at yourself."

Amy kept her smile in place, but it required real effort.

Dylan, she thought, must be laughing himself hoarse right about now at her naiveté—thinking that Honey's visit to the showrooms indicated a sincere desire to learn about Gavin's world of antiques and collectibles. *He could have warned me,* Amy thought. *Of course, then I'd have sent him—and he knew it.*

Sooner or later, she'd have her chance to pay him back for that. In the meantime, the basic question remained. If Honey thought that anything old was junk, and she obviously wasn't interested in any information which might challenge her belief, then why was she hanging around the showrooms, especially when Gavin wasn't there?

"How much is the mirror supposed to be worth?" Honey asked, and when Amy told her, she sniffed. "That's more than Gavin's paying for our entire honeymoon trip. And he says he can't afford any more than that—what a load of garbage that is. Surely he can spend the price of one little Italian mirror on an Italian honeymoon."

Amy saw the light and was surprised that it had taken her so long. "Of course Gavin doesn't get the whole amount," she pointed out. "The seller gets most of it."

Honey waved the objection away. "But he has all of these things to sell."

With that philosophy to deal with, Amy thought grimly, it was no wonder Gavin was feeling a financial pinch. "But you're scaling back all the plans now, aren't you?"

"I beg your pardon?"

"Because of the heart attack," Amy said. She felt as if she were talking to a kindergartner. "You'll have to postpone your trip, at the very least."

Honey looked at her blankly. "What gives you that idea? Gavin told me that his doctor wants him to have a long rest, so of course we'll be going."

Amy wondered if the doctor knew what Honey considered to be a restful agenda. But that would have to be decided between Gavin and Honey and the doctors. It certainly wasn't any of Amy's business.

"Getting away from it all will be the best thing for him," Honey went on. "In any case, he's already made all the deposits, and he won't want to waste the money."

But Amy wasn't listening. She'd been idly flipping the catalog pages back and forth, and suddenly her eye was caught by the photograph of a bed.

A carved and gilded George III four-poster bed, with the top rail and the headboard draped with heavy satin swags edged in deep fringe, with tassels at each corner.

She looked up from the black-and-white photo on the catalog page and saw the real thing standing halfway down the showroom floor. The satin swags were the color of heavy cream, and the fringe and tassels were gold.

But she had already known the colors. She'd have recognized it anywhere, because every Sunday morning of her childhood she had climbed into that bed to awaken her parents...

It was time for a new look, her mother had said. *There*

were a few things I didn't want to have around anymore.
Carol obviously hadn't done things halfway.

Amy didn't know why she should be surprised. Where
else would a no-longer-wanted George III bed end up
except in the Sherwood Auctions showroom? And surely
she should have anticipated that neither Carol nor Gavin
would particularly want that in-the-face reminder of their
marriage.

She hadn't cried in the three months since the
breakup. And everything considered, Amy told herself,
it was nothing short of stupid to break down over a bed.

But tears were stinging her eyelids anyway.

"It *is* horrible, isn't it?" Honey said, with a note of
ghoulish delight. "I can't imagine anyone wanting to
sleep in it. It's probably haunted."

By memories of happier days, Amy thought. But then
she could hardly expect Honey to appreciate that out-
look.

She heard Honey's voice as if from a distance. "Can
you believe Gavin asked if I wanted it? I told him not
to be ridiculous. How much is it worth, Amy? I do hope
it's a lot."

CHAPTER FOUR

BY THE time she finally ushered Honey back to the reception room and once more climbed the stairs all the way to the executive offices, it was almost noon and Amy was considering biting Dylan's head off the moment she saw him next. Why hadn't he warned her about Honey?

Though she supposed it was possible that she was being just slightly unfair to him, she conceded. Perhaps she shouldn't assume that Dylan had deliberately let her walk straight into that mess. She had concluded from his tone of voice that Honey wasn't precisely at the top of his list of people to see, but he hadn't actually said anything definite about the woman. So perhaps he had never seen her as clearly as Amy had just now in the showrooms, so he honestly hadn't thought there was any need of a warning.

If Honey had been careful when she was around him...

After all, Amy told herself, Gavin wasn't exactly the type to be easily taken in. So it was apparent that Honey could put on a very convincing act when she was with him—an act she hadn't bothered with today because she felt no need to impress Amy. Still, if she could keep Gavin convinced for all these months that she was adorable, how much easier it would it be for Honey to play the same trick on other men—men who weren't in such close contact with her as Gavin was. Men like Dylan.

On the other hand, Gavin—handicapped by his infatuation—would probably excuse all manner of slips from his darling, while a man like Dylan ought to be detached enough to see her more clearly. Which brought Amy back to the original argument—that he could have warned her, but hadn't.

Dylan wasn't in his office, though the page proofs of a catalog for an upcoming sale were scattered across his desk. The man had great instincts, Amy thought, to go out for lunch today of all days. So much for the idea of ordering in again and plunging once more into the list of prospective clients, picking his brain for any information he might have collected about the people she would be approaching. Of course, he'd had no idea of how long she'd be tied up with Honey. She herself had had no way of knowing that she would end up wasting half a day entertaining Honey, with nothing to show for it but smeared mascara and a touch of a headache.

Just as she pushed open the door of her own office, she heard the murmur of masculine voices from inside. *The moment I turn my back he's sitting in my chair. And he says he doesn't want the job.*

But this time Dylan hadn't taken over her desk. He was occupying an armchair in the small lounge area in the far corner of the room, and sitting opposite him was the man who had been ogling Honey in the waiting room when Amy went down to meet her.

Dylan rose as she came in. "There you are," he said. "I was just telling Mr. Benson that I hoped you'd be able to join us before long. Bill Benson, this is Amy Sherwood. Mr. Benson's mother died a few weeks ago, Amy."

Amy shook hands and sat down on the couch. "This must be a very difficult time for you."

Benson nodded curtly. "Yes—though she was nearly

ninety and she'd been in the nursing home for months, so it was hardly unexpected. The most difficult part is that now I'm left to deal with her odds and ends.''

''As the executor of his mother's estate, Mr. Benson would like us to take a look at her belongings and give him an opinion on what they would bring at auction,'' Dylan explained.

Odds and ends, Amy thought. No doubt it was a good description of the possessions of a ninety-year-old woman who had died in a nursing home. At least Bill Benson, unlike many people, didn't have delusions of getting rich from his mother's old stuff.

But how had he talked Robert into sending him all the way to the executive offices? There was a good reason for having separate departments, each with its own specialty, for no one person could possibly be an expert on everything. Besides, if every chance caller who wanted to sell a few excess possessions ended up closeted in the CEO's office—even if it was the CEO's personal assistant he was talking to instead of the head of the company—there would never be time to get ready for the big sales which had built the reputation of Sherwood Auctions.

That was probably why Dylan had called her in— because he was stuck and wanted her to be the bad guy and shift Benson to the appropriate department.

''We have some people on staff who specialize in valuing domestic goods,'' she began. ''In fact, we have a division that still does the old-fashioned kind of auction, selling an entire household right on the owner's front lawn. Perhaps someone from that department could be of more help than—''

Dylan interrupted. ''If we can visit the lady's house

this afternoon, her butler will be free to show us through.''

Butler? Amy felt her throat squeeze shut. She'd jumped wildly to a conclusion, based on Benson's attitude and two suggestive phrases—''odds and ends'' and ''nursing home''—and she'd nearly landed in quicksand. But if Mr. Benson's mother had hung onto both her house and her butler despite her need for nursing home care, then the chances were excellent that she'd owned silver for the butler to polish, a nice dining-room table for him to set…and who knew what else. No wonder Dylan hadn't taken the man downstairs to the household auction people….

''I'll have to check,'' she managed to say. ''But I think I can clear my calendar for the afternoon.''

''I can, too,'' Dylan said promptly.

Amy wasn't surprised. Bill Benson had been his discovery, after all—no wonder Dylan wanted to follow through. ''What's the deadline for that catalog copy?''

''First thing tomorrow, but I can take it home with me tonight to finish.''

''You're actually volunteering to work overtime?'' Amy murmured. She turned to Bill Benson. ''Shall we say two o'clock?''

Dylan opened his mouth as if to protest, but Benson stood up, cutting him off. ''I'll let Thomas know you're coming.'' He shook hands, and Dylan ushered him out of the office.

Amy was feeling light-headed. As soon as the men were out of earshot, she collapsed onto the couch, propping her feet high on the arm.

She was lying there with her eyes closed, fanning herself with her hand, when Dylan returned from reception a good ten minutes later. Without moving, she said, "We really need to work on our signals."

"That's for sure. I thought you were going to suggest he have a garage sale."

"The way he was talking, he made everything she owned sound like junk."

"I don't suppose it occurred to you to wonder how he got all the way up here."

He sounded a little abstracted, Amy thought. "Of course I wondered." She opened her eyes.

Dylan was looking at her legs. Belatedly she checked how far the hem of her skirt had slid up and decided that she was far from indecent. *Let him look.* "So tell me—how did he get up here, if he came in rattling about wanting to get rid of a bunch of odds and ends?"

"I heard him telling Robert about it when I went down to get the catalog copy from the messenger, and I was intrigued."

"You mean he was describing these odds and ends of his mother's better to Robert than he did to me?"

"Not exactly. I don't think he knows silver from stainless steel. But I did overhear the address—and a house located in the mansion section of Ward Parkway, complete with a butler, has to have something well worth looking at."

Amy gave a soundless whistle at the address. There were ritzier and more exclusive neighborhoods in Kansas City—but not many of them.

"I just can't believe you're willing to wait two hours to go see what's there," Dylan said.

That explained the protest he'd swallowed as Benson was leaving. "I didn't want to look too anxious. Drooling in front of a client is never good."

"I was more interested in setting the hook before the fish got away."

"Obviously. Offering to work tonight and everything...it takes my breath away." Amy sat up, rubbing her temples. "You know, I still can't help wondering if there's something wrong here."

"Not a chance. This is a prize."

"But the pieces of the story don't fit, Dylan. If she owned wonderful things, wouldn't her son know it? I mean, he might not appreciate them all, but he'd surely know they had value."

"Not necessarily. I say the place is a treasure trove. Want to put a bet on it?"

"Sure. How about a bottle of champagne?"

Dylan made a face. "Let's make it something interesting."

"Look, if I'm right, we'll use the champagne to drown our sorrows. If you're right, we'll pop it to celebrate." She held out a hand. "Shake on it?"

Dylan didn't answer, but he took her hand.

She felt a tingle which started in her fingertips and arced through her body till she could have mapped precisely where each nerve ran. She glanced up at him, expecting that the laughter in his eyes would help her get her balance back, but instead of humor she met an intense look which made her heart turn over.

"Maybe betting isn't such a good idea," she said, before she stopped to consider it.

Dylan's eyebrows lifted. "Having second thoughts already?"

"Nothing of the sort. I just thought—" *You're getting in deeper by the moment, Amy.* How could she possibly explain that odd flutter she'd felt? If she tried, and he got the wrong idea, things would be even more difficult.

He might even think she meant she was attracted to him, or something silly like that.

"Are you backing out because you're afraid you'll lose?"

"Of course not."

"That's what I thought. If you have any sense at all you want me to win this one, because you'd much rather lose a bottle of champagne than a good auction."

"It's just occurred to me that it isn't very professional to make a bet on something like that." She thought the excuse sounded incredibly lame, and judging by the tilt of Dylan's eyebrows he obviously agreed.

But he didn't argue the point. "Since you didn't want Benson to think you were overeager, you've left us with a couple of hours to kill."

"I thought you said that catalog copy was due to-morrow."

"Oh, I couldn't possibly concentrate on details when I'm suffering this kind of suspense. Let's go have lunch."

"Something tells me you don't have Chinese takeout in mind today."

"No, I was thinking more along the lines of Felicity's," Dylan said agreeably. "It's practically on the way. And don't forget it's your turn to buy."

Dylan hadn't paid much attention to her car that morning in the Plaza. He'd noticed that it was small and bright red, but he'd been too interested in other things—the way she looked in pink shorts, for one—to be too concerned about what she drove. But up close, Amy's sports car was smaller than it had looked earlier, and Dylan studied it warily before even trying to get in.

"If I throw my back out by folding myself up so I'll

fit in the passenger seat,'' he announced, ''I'm going to consider it a work-related injury. Where did you get this thing, anyway? As a prize in a cereal box?''

''Small cars have all kinds of advantages,'' Amy said. ''I can park anywhere, and my male friends never ask me if they can drive it.''

''That's only because they couldn't fit behind the wheel. If I go silent on you, Amy, I'm not being rude. It's just that having my knees pressed against my chest like this makes it hard to breathe.''

''I can go faster if you like,'' she offered, ''and maybe we can get to Felicity's before you pass out.''

''I don't think that would help. It's just a good thing Benson won't be expecting you to haul his mother's treasures out of the house today. Anything bigger than a pocket watch wouldn't fit.''

''*If* there are any treasures to be hauled.''

''Don't start that again.''

''Just because somebody has buckets of money doesn't mean they have good taste, Dylan. I've seen great houses in this town that have been furnished in early junkyard style.''

''You're just trying to dodge paying my bonus for discovering Bill Benson.''

''No, I'm afraid to get my hopes up.'' She sounded almost somber. ''After the mess with the Picasso and that abortive chat with Mitchell Harlow this morning, I'm not exactly in the running for best promoter of the year.''

''Look on the bright side. If the auction business doesn't work out, you can become a motivational speaker on the subject of dealing with rejection.''

''Thanks, you're very reassuring.'' She stopped the car in front of the valet station at Felicity's and turned to look at Dylan. "Are you getting out, or shall I ask if they'll provide curb service?"

Dylan groaned and pried himself out of the car.

"On second thought, maybe I should have checked to see if they have a table free before you went to all the effort of extracting yourself."

"They will. When I took Benson downstairs, I had Robert call for a reservation."

"It's a good thing *somebody* around there will do the secretarial stuff," Amy muttered.

The maître d' showed them to a table and Dylan glanced at the menu. "You might as well order the champagne right now."

"Sure of yourself, aren't you?"

"No, I'm just being helpful. If you're so uncomfortable with making a bet that you want to back out, let's just forget it. The bet, I mean—not the champagne."

"I'm not trying to back out, and I'm certainly not conceding. You're not getting champagne until you've earned it."

"That's the spirit," Dylan applauded. "I hate going up against an unworthy foe."

"Does nothing put a dent in your arrogance?"

He picked up the menu again and glanced at her over the top of it. She looked tired, he thought. Her mascara was smudged as if she'd rubbed her eyes without thinking of the consequences. Obviously she wasn't used to running at six in the morning.

Or was it more than that? When he looked more closely, he thought her eyelids looked ever so slightly pink. Had she been crying?

What kind of pressure was Gavin putting on her? Or was it something else?

He thought it over while she ordered, and then, when

he'd told the waiter what he wanted, he stirred sugar into his iced tea and said casually, "Speaking of arrogance, how was Honey this morning?"

She almost knocked over her glass. "So you have seen through her. Why didn't you warn me that she isn't interested in learning anything about antiques except what they're worth in today's market?"

"Because I didn't know it. I've only seen her in action with Gavin, when she appeared to be hanging on his every word."

"Well, she told me when I took her back to reception that she'd much rather tour the showrooms with me because I didn't lecture her with boring details like Gavin does. I just stuck to the important things—like estimated values."

"You two might become buddies yet—unless you intend to go running to Gavin and tell him what she's really like."

"As if that would do any good. He'd insist she was only teasing me, or tell me I'd misunderstood what she meant. And he'd be furious with me for interfering, because he's absolutely besotted with that woman. Even his being sick isn't going to delay the wedding. Not because Honey's so excited about being married—I think it's just that she's determined not to miss her trip to Italy."

The waiter brought their appetizer, and Dylan served a potato blini onto Amy's plate.

"Why Italy, anyway?" Amy asked suddenly. "A woman who hates anything old—why would she even think of going to Rome and Venice and Florence?"

"That's obvious. Designers. She's looking for clothes and shoes." How had she missed that angle, he wondered. She obviously knew clothes—if the suit she was wearing hadn't originated in Paris, it was the best knock-off he'd ever seen. Honey wouldn't have overlooked it, that was sure, and she'd have been green with envy.

Amy sighed. "You're right, I should have thought of that myself." She cut into the blini with a satisfying crunch. "Actually, what happened this morning just confirmed that I made the right choice three months ago when I resigned. If Honey's going to be involved at Sherwood Auctions after she marries Gavin—and from the look of things she'll definitely have her fingers in the pie, if only to keep track of the sales volume and the commissions—then I'm definitely going to be happier somewhere else. *Anywhere* else."

"Have you found that three-sided coin to flip yet?"

"No." She rubbed her temple almost fretfully, as if her head hurt. "And I forgot to call the university and the museum this morning. Honey blew everything else out of my mind."

"The university and the museum," he said thoughtfully, "but not the magazine."

"I talked to the editor last night, at the Maxwells' party. Though come to think of it, maybe I shouldn't close the door on the other two just yet."

"That sounds as if it's the magazine you really want to work for."

"If they're willing to wait for me." She smiled, but the expression didn't quite reach her eyes. "Roving expert—how could anyone turn that down?"

"It sounds like an impossible job."

"I wouldn't have to know everything as long as I know where to find things out and what questions to ask. I'd have a space each month to write about anything that intrigues me. It might be an unusual collection or a special collector, or the way to tell whether the oil painting you unearthed in the attic is worth taking to an appraiser. Or how to clean silverplate without ruining it.''

''It sounds just like going back to school.''

''But that's it exactly! That's what I like so much about the auction business, too. Every day is different— every sale, every client. You just never know what will turn up in the showroom next.'' She bit her lip, and he wondered what was coming. ''Dylan—you know the George III bed that's on display right now?''

''Yeah.'' Just the reminder was enough to make him feel irritable. ''That's the one that practically gave me ulcers because Gavin insisted it had to go into this sale, even if it meant tearing up the catalog and starting over.''

''Did you?''

''Tear up the catalog? No, at the last minute I was able to rearrange some pages and make room to fit it in.''

''Why was he so anxious to get it into this sale?''

''I didn't ask. Probably because it might be a while before he collects another group of furniture that'll draw the really high-caliber buyers. Or maybe the seller was anxious to have cash in hand.''

''No doubt,'' she said. She sounded a little bitter.

''Amy, if there's some mystery about this bed—''

''Didn't he tell you? It belonged to him and my mother.''

Dylan winced. ''I didn't know. It just showed up a couple of weeks ago, and I was more concerned with getting the printers to cooperate than in wondering where it came from.''

''I see why neither of them wants it,'' Amy said.

''Well yes, under the circumstances. But why not give it to you?''

"Have you looked at that thing? The real bed, I mean, not just the photograph of it. They had to raise the ceiling in their bedroom to make room for it. It would never fit in my apartment." She sniffed. "Still, it would have been nice if they'd asked me."

"Maybe you should be glad they didn't," Dylan said. "Honey would have wanted to charge you full price."

Amy's first glance at the Benson house on Ward Parkway told her that Dylan's instincts were very good. The mansion looked as if it had been there forever. Tudor in style and enormous in size, it was surrounded by mature trees and shrubs, and it looked out from its corner location at an angle across the expanse of green space which separated the lanes of the wide street.

As Amy parked her car in the circle drive in front of the house, Dylan looked dreamily up at the brick facade and murmured, "As champagne goes, I generally prefer Dom Pérignon."

"I'm glad to know that," she said crisply. "You may still be the one who's buying it."

"Game to the last, aren't you, Amy? You're a sport, I have to grant you."

He rang the bell and stood politely aside so that she could get the first glimpse inside when the butler answered.

When Amy looked quizzically at him, he said, "It's not that I don't want to see for myself. I'm just confident." He reached into his pocket. "In fact, here's my handkerchief so you can mop up the drool."

The butler was elderly and white-haired, and his shoulders were slightly stooped. He took the business card Amy held out and stepped silently back to let them in. "Mr. Benson said you'd like to see everything," he murmured. "I shall do my best. Follow me, please."

Amy was already looking past him to an arts-and-crafts display case. Though the style of the piece clashed horribly with the architecture of the staircase behind it, it was a lovely bit of furniture—and if the china inside wasn't Staffordshire, she'd eat it on the spot.

"Judging by that smile," Dylan said in her ear, "a regular bottle of champagne isn't nearly enough. For this, you should make it a magnum. Or wait, there's a bottle that's bigger yet. I just can't remember what it's called."

"Don't count your chickens, Copeland. You're barely past the front door."

His eyebrows lifted. "But Amy, sweetheart, that's exactly my point. Just think of the treasures yet to be unearthed."

The butler led the way into the large living room. "Like that, for instance?" Amy murmured. She didn't point; she didn't need to.

Dylan followed her gaze to a table and chairs that looked as if it had come straight out of her grandmother's kitchen—except, if the set had been owned by Edith Sherwood, it wouldn't have been in such sad shape. The tubular steel legs of the set were flecked with rust and the plastic coating on the top had peeled off two corners, as if it had stood outdoors, unprotected from the weather, for a considerable period.

Dylan didn't say a word. Amy, glancing at him, saw that he was staring in disbelief not at the table but at the frame above the carved marble mantel. She couldn't see it clearly from where she was standing; the light reflected oddly from the surface of the art.

The butler said, "That's the mistress's puzzle table. She enjoyed her jigsaws until her sight began to fail."

"I should say she did," Dylan muttered.

Amy moved a couple of steps and looked again at the heavy, obviously expensive frame he was studying. No wonder she hadn't been able to see it clearly; the shiny printed surface was broken by rows of twisting cracks. It wasn't a piece of art at all that Bill Benson's mother had framed in heavy gold and hung above her mantel. It was a gigantic jigsaw puzzle—a picture of an oversize hamburger, complete with sesame seed bun, ketchup and pickle slices.

Amy felt a bubble of irrational laughter rising inside her at the look on Dylan's face. But since she could hardly give way to hysterical amusement at the moment, she forced herself to look around the room instead. Next to the steel and plastic table stood a Victorian love seat and several matching chairs upholstered in deep purple plush—not an unusual parlor set, but a nicely preserved one. Across from them, however, was a truly lovely carved Gothic chair that must be three hundred years old.

Amy's head was beginning to spin at the contrasts.

The plate rail running round the top of the dining room was lined with gorgeous plates. Mostly Spode, Amy thought, with a sprinkling of Meissen. A china cabinet at one end of the room held something she thought would turn out to be Sevres, though it would take the expert eye of Beth Gleason to be certain. But the hutch at the far end was full of mass-produced pottery and cheap, heavy glass.

She was running a hand over the surface of the dining-room table when the doorbell pealed. The butler excused himself.

"This woman didn't buy antiques," Amy said, "she

must have bought entire stores—and hauled all the contents home, regardless of quality. Have you ever seen such a crazy mix of stuff?''

''She certainly had eclectic tastes.''

''Or a split personality. Everything in here is either absolutely wonderful or it's junk. There's nothing ordinary.''

The butler returned, with Bill Benson following him. ''I came by to see how the tour is going,'' he said.

''Your mother had some truly lovely pieces,'' Amy said. ''We'd be honored if you'd allow us to select items from her collection to auction.''

Bill Benson frowned and turned to Dylan instead. ''But I want to get rid of everything.''

''Of course,'' Amy said. ''And we can do that. The cream of the collection, like this china and the Gothic chair in the living room, will go into our premiere auctions. Of course, that leaves quite a lot of everyday things, the sort of belongings we all collect—and those would probably sell better in a neighborhood auction. I'll need to have a number of our employees come through the house, appraising items and deciding what should be moved to the auction house and what should be left in place for sale here.''

Bill Benson looked unhappy. ''I wanted to get this over right away.''

''We can act fairly quickly, Mr. Benson. I completely understand why you don't want the process drawn out—''

The doorbell rang again, and the butler vanished silently down the hallway.

''I assure you we'll do the best and speediest job we can,'' Amy went on. ''But I must point out that speed isn't the only objective. We also want you to get the maximum price for each piece, and sometimes that means a delay so we can properly advertise and—''

A loud bang from the front of the house made them all jump. ''The wind must have caught the front door,'' Dylan said.

But that's a very heavy door, Amy thought. *There isn't enough wind today to push it around.*

Footsteps thudded down the hall toward the dining room.

As one, they all turned to face the tall, bulky woman who stood on the threshold, glaring at Bill Benson. ''I should have known you'd try to pull a fast one,'' she accused. ''Selling all this—even though it isn't yours to sell.''

CHAPTER FIVE

THE air in the dining room suddenly seemed to have grown oppressively hot, and everything Amy looked at had a faint greenish tinge around the edges.

This can't be happening, she thought. *Not another one.*

The woman in the doorway rounded on Amy and Dylan. "So you're the auction people," she said. "Well, let me tell you about Billy here—my little worm of a stepbrother with the gigantic power complex."

"How did you even know about this, Hattie?" Bill Benson asked.

"Oh, I've been stopping by every day to talk to Thomas, because I've been expecting you to pull something of the sort. When he told me you'd asked him to show these people through the house, I knew it was time to intervene. Whatever makes you think—"

Within moments, the two were screaming accusations at each other, but Amy was too stunned to take in all the details. *Three strikes and you're out,* she told herself wearily. The Picasso. Mitchell Harlow. And now this.

Dylan, on the other hand, seemed to be enjoying the scene. He stood in the middle of the dining room with his arms folded across his broad chest, looking back and forth with the same sort of casual intentness he'd display if he was watching an interesting tennis match. Finally, in the midst of the shouting, he said, "Let's sit down and discuss this sensibly, shall we?"

He said it almost quietly, but to Amy's astonishment,

the timbre of his voice cut easily across the squabble, the screaming abruptly stopped and, after a moment of stunned silence, the two combatants pulled out chairs at the dining-room table.

Amy noticed that Dylan automatically took the armchair at the head of the table—and it was obvious that neither Bill Benson nor his stepsister even considered challenging him for it. Amy wasn't surprised; she was still almost speechless herself at the effortless way he'd sliced through the quarrel. *No wonder Gavin makes his own phone calls.*

While the two combatants were still settling themselves, separated by the width of the table, she took the chair at Dylan's right hand. "What do you think you're doing?"

"Trying my damnedest," he said under his breath, "to save my bottle of champagne." He looked from Bill Benson to the woman. "Let me review the situation, to make sure I've got the details straight, and then we'll move on to finding a compromise."

The woman sniffed as if the possibility seemed too remote to consider.

Dylan ignored her and turned to Benson. "I gather that this was your mother's second marriage. And you—" He turned to the woman. "Your father was Mrs. Benson's second husband?"

"They were married just two years," she said almost sullenly, "when he died. That's been five years ago. My father wanted me to have my share, but she insisted everything was hers to use as long as she liked. Then, when she wrote her will, she named her son as executor, and he thinks that means he can do anything he likes with every single item in this house."

"You, naturally enough, want the things that belonged to your father."

Hattie nodded. "I want the Meissen china, the silver tea service, the gothic chair, the pier mirror on the land-ing—"

Amy found herself nodding. It seemed fair enough for Hattie to have what had belonged to her father. And the late-in-life combination of households certainly ex-plained not only the misfit collections—museum pieces standing next to pure kitsch—but the sense she'd had that Bill Benson didn't have a clue what his mother's "odds and ends" really included. Even now, he obvi-ously didn't see why those things should be so important to his stepsister—but if they weren't valuable to him, why was he making such a fuss about giving her what she wanted?

Benson interrupted. "She's making me out to be a thief, and I'm not. I don't care what she takes—it would be that much less hassle for me to deal with. But the other two will never agree."

"The other two?" Amy asked blankly. "The other two *what?*"

Hattie said stiffly, "My half sisters, one each from my father's second and third marriages. Mrs. Benson was actually his fourth wife."

"But you see, the two of them also want the dishes," Benson said, "and—what else were you demanding I hand over? Oh, yeah—the tea set and the mirror and that ridiculously uncomfortable chair. Except they wanted a whole lot of other stuff, too. But then, to be fair, Hattie here was just getting started on her list, so it might turn out to be every bit as long as theirs."

"I see," Amy muttered. She pressed her index fingers to her temples, where veins were beginning to throb.

"In fact, Sylvia had me paged at the funeral home just as the services started," Benson explained, "and told me if either of the others got anything that was on her list she'd sue me for mishandling the estate. Emma at least waited till after the funeral was over, but her list was so long she faxed it to me. She said she did it so I couldn't pretend I'd forgotten anything she claimed."

"And now Hattie wants the same items," Dylan mused.

"You got it. That's why I decided the only sensible way was to auction everything before they could find out about the sale, split the money, and be done with it." He settled back in his chair, arms folded across his chest, jaw thrust out pugnaciously.

There was a long silence.

As a plan for keeping peace among the siblings, it wasn't exactly the most promising Amy had ever heard. But she couldn't fault Bill Benson for preferring to have the whole thing over with, whatever the cost, rather than make an effort to do what was obviously impossible— create a settlement that was not only fair to all but which would keep everyone in this fractious family happy.

"I think Mr. Benson has a point," Amy said slowly. "An auction is the only way to divide things satisfactorily."

"Of course you'd think that," Hattie said with an almost-cordial smile, "since it's the only way you stand to make any money. But if you think for an instant that I'm going to step aside and watch my family heirlooms knocked down to the highest bidder at a public auction, or worse yet actually stand on the front lawn and make bids on my own inheritance—"

"I didn't say anything about a public auction," Amy pointed out. "What I'm suggesting is that we bring in a

crew to inventory the entire house, and then send a copy
of the inventory to each heir so you can look at the list,
think it over, and decide which items are most important
to you. When you've all had a chance to do that, you
can set a time, at your convenience, to meet here, and
we'll go through the list so you can all bid on the items
you want.''

Hattie was frowning. "You mean like bidding with
play money?''

"Not quite," Amy said. "Whatever you bid is considered part of your share of the final payout when the
estate's settled, so if you buy a lot of stuff, then you'll
get less cash in the end. You might even end up owing
money to the estate, if you want a lot of the material
goods. That's oversimplified, of course, but—''

Benson said, "And then it would be over?''

Amy nodded. "It could all be finished in a matter of
a few weeks. The inventory would take a while, but our
staff is very efficient.''

Dylan, she saw, was staring at her. Then he shook his
head as if to clear it and addressed Benson and Hattie.
"We'd have to charge you for the time involved in the
inventory and the actual auction, of course.''

"But not a commission on the sales price, as we
would at a public auction," Amy added.

Benson and Hattie looked at each other.

"It might work," she said finally. "I'll call Sylvia
and Emma.''

Amy pushed her chair back. "Let us know if you want
to proceed," she said.

Dylan followed her outside.

As she started the car, Amy took a deep breath.
"There goes another possibility down the drain. Three
in less than twenty-four hours—that's got to be a record.

Plus I can't wait to hear what Gavin has to say about me committing staff to inventory an entire house without even getting an auction out of the deal.''

Dylan twisted round to get more comfortable. "He wasn't there, so you can't let his opinion bother you.''

Easy for you to say, Amy thought. "Maybe I'll be lucky and they won't call back.''

"Oh, they'll call. What other choices do they have? Anyway, I suspect Gavin would have done the same thing. He'd have been the first one to think of the goodwill it'll create for the auction company if we can settle their family squabble.''

"That's a big *if.* What was I thinking of, not to run?''

"But even if Sherwood Auctions doesn't make much money from the Battling Bensons—''

"They're not all named Benson," Amy pointed out. "They can't be.''

"True. But trust me, I don't want to get to know them well enough to sort out the last names. At any rate, we probably prevented a couple of homicides today. Call it our contribution to society.''

Amy was almost silent on the drive back to the office, and Dylan decided not to press the subject. For that matter, he didn't much want to wallow in discussion of what had happened this afternoon, either. He'd taken Bill Benson at face value, which had not only been an egregious misstep but was a folly that Amy had not stumbled into. In this case, he reflected, her instincts had been a great deal better than his. But instead of him listening to her, his pride had insisted he was right. So he hadn't asked the few additional questions that would have saved everybody a lot of trouble.

Trouble that Amy, in particular, hadn't needed. No wonder she was discouraged, after the day she'd had.

"I owe you a bottle of champagne," he said. "We could go drown our sorrows in it right now."

"No, thanks. I'm already depressed enough, and I promised my mother that I'd stop by the house tonight."

"That sounds like a cheerful finish to the day."

A humorless smile flickered briefly on her lips. "I can think of things I'd rather do today than explain to my mother how I happened to end up working for Gavin again."

Instead of parking in the employee lot, Amy pulled her car in beside the curb at the front door of Sherwood Auctions and left the engine running. Dylan opened the passenger door but didn't get out. "You could volunteer to stay late and help me proofread the catalog copy. I'll call Carol and tell her you can't come after all."

"I don't do catalog copy," she said sweetly.

Dylan wondered how long she'd been waiting for the chance to quote his own words back at him. At least there was some actual amusement in her voice this time, but it didn't last long.

"So far," she mused, "not feeling responsible for that particular duty is the only good thing I've found about being the boss."

Dylan closed the door again and twisted around in his seat to look more closely at her. "You're really singing the blues, aren't you?"

"Wouldn't you be? Maybe I should go talk to Gavin. If I confess what a dead loss I've been so far, maybe he'll do what he should have done in the first place and put you in charge."

Dylan shook his head. "I told you, Amy, I'm not interested."

"But that was because you thought I'd try to dodge any trouble by putting the blame on you. If I tell Gavin the truth, then I won't be pretending to be the boss anymore and you'd be entirely free to act. You might even like the job if I'm not around."

Not a chance, he thought. *Without you around it would be a lot less amusing.*

Her hands twisted restlessly on the steering wheel.

"I know everything seems to be going wrong at the moment," he said. "But it's not your fault, Amy. If the Maxwells and Mitchell Harlow had been such sure things, Gavin would have had agreements locked up weeks ago. The Picasso would be sitting in the showroom and we'd be busily authenticating autographs."

She didn't answer, and she didn't look at him.

He put his hand on her shoulder. The muscles which lay under his fingertips were taut and hard. Slowly and gently, he rubbed, trying to relax the tight ridges.

She bent her neck a little and a lock of dark hair slid over her shoulder, caressing the back of his hand. It felt like warm silk—slick and almost weightless. Without conscious thought, he raised his hand, letting his fingertips slide through the soft curtain until his palm cupped the back of her head and turned her face toward him.

Her eyes, huge and dark, acted on him like a magnet. He leaned toward her, so close that he could feel the quick warmth of her breath against his face. He focused on her mouth just as the tip of her tongue lightly moistened her lips.

She turned her head abruptly and his lips brushed the soft curve of her cheek.

"This isn't any way to finish up a catalog," she said. There was an odd catch in her voice that might have been anger—or something else altogether.

She was right, and he knew it. What the devil was he thinking, anyway? "I'll see you tomorrow, Amy."

She nodded, and the moment he was out of the car it sped away.

He held the main door for Beth Gleason, who was coming out, and went into the building. At the reception desk, Robert looked past him and said, "There's a phone call for Ms. Sherwood. Is she—"

"She won't be back this afternoon," Dylan said. Robert released the lock on the inner door and he went through into the main lobby.

A murmur came from the showrooms but he ignored it and went on up to the executive suite. He was used to the office being quiet and dark when he came in, but this time it felt emptier than usual.

Without you around it would be a lot less amusing.

The admission had passed through his mind so quickly that at the time he hadn't even registered what he'd been thinking. Only now did the words come back to pester him.

What had come over him, trying to kiss her? And what had happened to the very sensible promise he'd made himself just yesterday—to keep his distance from Amy Sherwood?

When Amy arrived at the house in Hyde Park where she'd grown up, her mother was kneeling in a flower bed next to the front steps. When she saw Amy, Carol Sherwood shook the loose earth from her trowel and gathered up a basket and a tray full of seedlings. "I wasn't expecting you quite yet," she called.

Amy walked across the lawn. "Don't stop on my account. Those plants look as if they need to be in the dirt."

"They'd be happier. If you're not in a hurry—"

"I'm not." From her handbag came a tinny melody and she dug out her cell phone. "At least, I have the evening free unless this is an emergency." She pushed a button. "Amy Sherwood."

"This is Brad Parker," said the editor of *Connoisseur's Choice.*

Amy caught her breath. She'd tried to put the magazine out of her mind, but all of her hopes and fears came rushing back at the sound of his voice.

"I caught up with the publisher today."

She tried not to sound breathless. "So soon? And what did Mr. Dougal say?"

"He told me to wait a couple of weeks for you before I fill that position. Only a couple of weeks, mind. But if you're still interested under those conditions—"

A reprieve, Amy thought. Of course, two weeks wasn't much—but she'd simply have to make sure it was enough. If she could just pull in a contract or two, then surely she could turn things over to Dylan, no matter what his objections. Or maybe by then Gavin would be back on the job...

Determination steeled her voice. "I'm interested, Brad."

"Then stop by when you have a chance and we'll work out the details."

She put the telephone away. Maybe she should go back to the office tonight, and push a little harder to find a solution to Gavin's problems.

Carol hadn't stopped planting. Her fingers worked nimbly, fitting each tiny seedling into a hole and pressing earth closely around it.

Amy got a second kneeling pad from the huge gardening basket and put it down at the edge of the flower bed. "I'll help, if you hand me some of those seedlings." The cool earth felt good on her fingers, and she looked at the tiny plants instead of at her mother. "I suppose you'd like to know why I was answering the phone at the auction house this morning."

"Only if you want to tell me," Carol said calmly. "It seems to me it's a matter between you and Gavin."

"You aren't angry?"

"That you've gone back to work for him? I don't think it's any of my business. But I'm glad you're not holding a grudge against your father anymore."

Amy dropped the seedling. Carol sounded perfectly sincere, but surely—"I'm only filling in for a short while, until he's back to work."

"I see. Well, that shouldn't be long. A few weeks of rest and he'll be good as new."

"Unless Honey has her way." The words were out before Amy paused to consider if it was wise to say anything about the woman who had replaced Carol in Gavin's life.

But Carol didn't grow red, or shout, or even flinch. "She doesn't want him to go back to work at all?" She sounded mildly interested.

"No. I mean it seems she doesn't want him to rest. She's still planning a wedding trip to Italy—"

Carol tipped her head to one side and said thoughtfully, "She's very young, you know."

"Just a year older than I am. It's enough to make me spit nails. Mother, I don't understand. Aren't you upset about any of it?"

Carol sat back on her heels and looked at Amy. "For one thing, Gavin's health is not my concern any longer."

"But you've been calling Dylan every day to ask about him."

"Yes. But I'd do the same for a friend I'd known for thirty years. And if you're worried about me because I'm not planning revenge, or gloating over what's happened to him—well, I decided all that was a waste of energy. I'd rather plant flowers." She held up a seedling. "This is one of my favorites, but it's a variety that always made your father sneeze."

"So now you can have them."

"As many as I want." Carol tucked another plant into the earth. "And if we're talking about blame where this divorce is concerned—"

"You weren't the one who was cheating." Amy's voice had a hard edge.

"No, I wasn't. And I was furious when he confessed and asked for the divorce. But once I had time to think about it, I realized that the fact is Honey didn't break up the marriage. She was only the end, the culmination."

"If you're going to tell me you've been miserable all these years, Mother—"

"No, darling. Nothing so dramatic, I'm afraid. We'd simply grown apart, and that was as much my fault as Gavin's. We'd stopped working on being a couple." She put the last seedling in. "There. A little water and they'll be all tucked in. You know, the one thing I do begrudge Honey is that trip to Italy. All these years I've wanted to travel, but Gavin's always been too busy at the auction house."

Amy, still stunned, said, "Maybe you should take a cruise around the world."

"Perhaps I should," Carol mused. "Once all the financial arrangements are complete, I'll have plenty of money for things like that."

I certainly hope so, Amy thought.

"Somehow I never liked the idea of traveling alone,

but I'm learning I can do all sorts of things by myself. So why not that, too? Thanks, Amy. I'll have to decide where I want to go first.''

Amy opened her mouth to suggest that Carol not buy any tickets just yet, and then she realized how much she'd have to explain if she said anything of the sort. She'd have to explain Gavin's financial crisis, and the reason she'd agreed to return to Sherwood Auctions. Better just to leave things as they were, and not risk upsetting the peace Carol had found for herself.

''In the meantime,'' Carol said, ''let's go wash up and make ourselves a salad.''

There were two messages waiting for Amy when she arrived at Sherwood Auctions the next morning. Bill Benson and his stepsister had each called to tell her that they wanted to proceed with her plan for a family auction. ''It's as if they didn't trust each other enough even to get the message straight,'' she told Dylan. ''Do you want to be in charge of the inventory team?''

He leaned back in his chair and studied her thoughtfully. ''Do I look like the type who enjoys being tortured?''

''Well, that's a change. At least you didn't tell me you're not a secretary so you don't do inventories.''

''Only because you're learning so well that you don't need to be reminded. Besides, the whole family auction thing was your idea, not mine.''

''Don't rub it in, Copeland.'' She started for the door.

''The furniture that's in the showroom now is due to be auctioned this weekend.''

She paused. ''And?''

''Are you going to be starting off the sale yourself?''

Amy sighed. She hadn't thought nearly that far ahead.

With the pressure she'd been under, the weekend had seemed an eternity away.

She had also managed to conveniently forget how Gavin had always taken pride in the individual touch by starting out each auction at the podium, personally taking bids. During important auctions he often kept the gavel all the way through the evening. And the furniture sale should be one of their biggest of the year. Gavin would not have delegated it, and in his absence, their patrons would be expecting his stand-in.

She nodded. "Just make sure I have the order of sale and all the price information—targets and reserves— early. Gavin may be able to glance at those things and memorize them, but I'll have to study."

When? a little voice at the back of her mind asked.

She took the back stairs to Beth Gleason's office and found her inspecting a vase through a jeweler's loupe, studying each inch of the surface for possible damage. Amy settled into a chair and waited patiently till Beth was finished. "That's the ugliest vase I've ever laid eyes on."

"You won't think so when you see the price it brings. It may be ugly, but it's also one of a kind."

"That's because nobody could stand looking at two of them."

"What's the matter? Have you already forgotten Gavin's lecture about how everything that moves through this building is beautiful?" Beth put the loupe away and sat down behind her desk. "How are things upstairs?" A half smile tugged at the corner of her mouth.

"Challenging. How would you like to take on a special assignment?" Amy pulled her feet up on the edge of the chair, wrapped her arms around her knees, and told Beth about the Battling Bensons.

"Inventory only," she finished. "Just rough appraisals, though you might keep a list of anything that's outstanding, because if no one in the family wants it we'll probably end up selling it for them."

"So basically you want me to go through the house and stick a number on everything, then make a list."

"Not by yourself," Amy added hastily. "You can have as big a team as you need to get the job done in a hurry."

Beth sighed. "Sure, I don't have anything better to drive myself crazy with this week. And it sounds as if the Battling Bensons have to be seen to be believed."

"Good. Can you go over there today and take a quick look? Then you'll have a better idea of who you'll need to help you out, to be sure of getting an accurate inventory."

Beth nodded. "I can go this morning. Who's going to run the actual auction?"

"Dylan and I will, I suppose."

"Too bad it won't be open to onlookers—it could be quite a show." Beth shot a sideways glance at Amy. "Sort of like the one I watched in front of the building yesterday."

Amy's face felt as if it were freezing.

"A word to the wise, Amy," Beth murmured. "Next time you plan to canoodle with Dylan Copeland in broad daylight, you might not want to park right by the main entrance."

Amy took the stairs again, hoping that the climb would give her time to recover her composure—or at least give her a reason for being pink in the face when she got back to her office. In truth, she was still warm with embarrassment.

She should have held onto her dignity and not said a word. She should certainly not have tried to explain to Beth what had actually happened in her car yesterday—which of course, could be summed up in one word. *Nothing.* But of course Beth hadn't believed that, and Amy should have known that she wouldn't. If she had only stopped to think for an instant, she would have realized that explaining would only make it seem as if she had something to hide.

But she hadn't stopped to think. Instead she had rushed into words—and Beth had listened politely with a half smile which said louder than words that she didn't buy a line of Amy's account. *Accidental indeed,* she seemed to be saying.

Finally Beth had picked up the ugly vase again and held it up to the light. "Look," she said, "it's no shame to be caught kissing him. In fact, I'd say it's something to be proud of. Every unattached woman in this building—and a few who'd like to trade up—have been trying to get Dylan's attention since the first day he came to work here."

"I never did," Amy said before she could stop herself.

"Maybe you weren't throwing yourself at him like some of them were, but if he'd given you any encouragement—"

That was when Amy had walked out and started up the stairs—because Beth was correct, up to a point. Amy hadn't thrown herself at Dylan, but she'd been interested. Which was more than Dylan had been.

But she could have climbed all the way to heaven and it wouldn't have been far enough; she was still indignant—mostly at herself—when she reached the executive floor.

Dylan looked up as she came in. "Where'd you get the sunburned face?" he asked.

"None of your business." She started for her own office. "I don't want to be disturbed for the rest of the morning. No phone calls, no visitors. I'm going to closet myself with that stack of folders and find somebody who wants to auction something."

"Amy—"

She stopped in midstep and let out a long, irritated breath that was so forceful it ruffled her bangs. "I know, you're not a secretary so you don't intercept phone calls and visitors."

"You already have one waiting for you. A visitor, not a phone call."

She looked toward the almost-closed door of her office. She lowered her voice, but there was a sharp edge to it nonetheless. "You brought someone up here and let them wait in my office, with all the confidential stuff that's lying on my desk?"

"I moved your folders out here. And the drawers of that desk creak, so if he was snooping I'd have known it. He's been reading a magazine for half an hour."

"I still don't appreciate—"

"I brought him up here because I thought you'd rather have him waiting for you alone in your office instead of sitting downstairs, where he could change his mind at any moment and walk out."

Amy considered. "If by that you mean he's got something to sell, yes. But I'm warning you, this had better not be another Bill Benson."

"Scout's honor," Dylan said.

She pushed the door open.

Sitting on the couch with a copy of *Connoisseur's Choice* open on the coffee table in front of him was Mitchell Harlow.

He turned a page. "Ms. Sherwood," he said. "Ever since we went running yesterday, I've been thinking about what you said about how I never look at my autograph collection anyway and how I could sort of trade it in for something valuable. And I have a question. Do you really think I could get enough money out of my autographs to buy both a yacht and a Lamborghini?"

CHAPTER SIX

FOR one wild instant, Amy wanted to run across the room, throw her arms around Mitchell Harlow, and kiss him. He might be an unlikely looking knight—dressed in a brown suit and a garish necktie instead of in shining armor, brandishing an autograph collection instead of a sword and shield. But he was certainly riding to the rescue of this damsel in distress.

Then sanity reasserted itself, and prudence followed. Besides, she noted from the corner of her eye, Dylan had followed her into the room. He was carrying a clipboard, but that didn't fool her for an instant—he wasn't planning to take notes, he just wanted to listen in on the conversation. If the tables had been turned, she'd have tried to listen in, too.

She crossed the room and perched on the edge of the wing chair opposite Mitchell. "A yacht *and* a Lamborghini?" she said cautiously. "Well, maybe not both. Those are pretty expensive toys."

He looked disappointed. "But you said—"

From his position behind Mitchell, Dylan rolled his eyes skyward.

Amy scrambled to retrieve her position before Dylan could step in, and before Mitchell could get the notion that if he didn't end up with both a boat and a sports car it would hardly be worth selling the autograph collection at all.

"You see," she explained, "I don't know exactly what the autographs would bring at auction. Nobody ever knows what an item is really worth until it actually goes under the hammer and the buyers set a value. So estimates are really only educated guesses at best. But if what I've been told about the collection is correct, I don't think you'll be disappointed. Do you really have the signature of Catherine the Great?''

Mitchell shrugged. ''How should I know what I've got? Most of those things are such scrawls nobody can read them.''

That didn't sound particularly promising, Amy thought. Surely a collection with real value would have been organized, marked, and inventoried so that the most cursory look would make it plain that it was out of the ordinary. If it had been handed down in the family, someone must have cared enough to keep track of the details and make sure it wouldn't be carelessly destroyed by someone who didn't recognize its value. Or did Mitchell's offhand comment simply mean that he had never done more than take a casual glance?

''I'd have to look at the collection,'' she said firmly, ''before I could begin to take a guess on the value.''

Mitchell brightened again. ''You want to look at my autographs?''

''That would be the place to start, yes. I assume the collection is in a bank vault?'' She glanced at her watch. ''We could go to your bank right now, unless we need to make an appointment.''

''Oh, no,'' Mitchell said earnestly. ''It's at my apartment. I always keep it there.''

Even though you seldom look at it? Amy swallowed hard. *Even though it's supposed to be nearly priceless?* But it was a little late to lecture him about security and proper care. If he had anything worth selling, she would insist that part of the deal must be to let her move the autographs to a safer place—immediately. "When would be a good time for me to look at the collection?"

"How about coming over tonight?" he said. "If you're free, that is."

She almost asked if they couldn't make it sooner, and then remembered her own advice about not looking too anxious. Besides, though she wasn't sure what Mitchell Harlow did for a living, he'd already interrupted his day by coming to talk to her—and he hadn't volunteered to give up another hour or two just now.

"I'll make a point of being free whenever it's convenient for you," she said.

He beamed at her so brightly that she felt a bit lost, like a student who had stumbled across the right answer and been rewarded for it, but who still didn't quite understand the question. "And I'll need your address."

When he told her, Amy felt a little better about him keeping a valuable collection in his apartment, because the tower where he lived—the same one where the Maxwells kept their Picasso—probably had the tightest security in the city. "I'll stop by this evening," she said.

"I'll tell the doorman you'll be visiting." Mitchell stood up.

"Is there any particular time you'd like us to come?" Dylan asked.

Mitchell looked at him levelly. "I didn't realize you were so interested in autographs, Copeland."

"I'm interested in everything," Dylan said. His tone was gentle, but Amy thought she could hear an edge underlying the softness.

"We'll decide later whether you need to come, Dylan," Amy said hastily. "I'll walk you down, Mitchell."

In the reception room, he said, "I'll expect you about

seven o'clock.'' Instead of shaking the hand she offered, he pressed it between his own.

When she got back upstairs, Dylan was sitting on his desk, looking into space. ''Do you want to meet there, or shall I pick you up?''

''You really hate riding in my car, don't you?'' Amy didn't wait for an answer. ''You know, I think maybe I'd better handle this one on my own. For now, at least.''

His eyebrows raised just a fraction. ''I thought we were stuck in this together.''

''Yes, but you keep telling me you don't want the responsibility of being the boss. Well, if the buck stops on my desk, then I get to make the decisions.'' She started to pace his office. ''And I don't think it would be a good idea for you to go tonight. I don't know what's going on between you and Mitchell Harlow—''

''Don't you?'' His voice was very silky.

''But he seems to want to deal with me, and this is just too important for me to take a chance on anything upsetting him. It's bad enough that I don't know much about autographs, but unless you're an expert—''

''I don't claim to be, no.''

''Then I don't think you'd be much help with a preliminary assessment. That's the problem with being generalists in the auction business. We have to know enough about everything to recognize the valuable stuff, so there's no time to specialize.''

''I read somewhere that a signature which says 'Elizabeth I' is always a fraud,'' Dylan said helpfully.

Amy stopped pacing for a moment to look at him in astonishment. ''Of course it is. How could she have known there'd be another Elizabeth someday?''

''And Attila the Hun didn't sign his name like that.''

"Mostly because 'Hun' wasn't his last name. Or could he even write at all? I can't remember."

"Maybe he made an *X*."

"Doubtful. I wonder what the equivalent would have been, back then." Amy started pacing again. "I'm just awfully afraid that's what this collection is going to be—documents plainly dated 37 B.C., a letter from Socrates written in modern English, and other assorted impossibilities."

"You're a pessimist, Amy."

"That's humorous, coming from the guy who unearthed the Battling Bensons."

"Touché."

"Anyway, I'm not exactly pessimistic. It's just that I'm afraid to get my hopes up too high. For one thing, I shudder to think of the condition that collection may be in from just sitting around Mitchell Harlow's apartment all this time instead of being stored in a climate-controlled vault."

"It's not a good sign," Dylan agreed.

"And it means that either Mitchell is exceptionally naive to keep an almost-priceless set of autographs at home under less than optimal conditions, or Gavin was misled about what the collection included and it's really not valuable at all." She stopped in the middle of the room. "Here's your chance to get even, Dylan. Do you want to go double or nothing on that bottle of champagne?"

"It depends on which way you're betting."

"The way my week has been going, I'm betting that Gavin was wrong."

Dylan shook his head. "Not interested. I'd have to be crazy to take the other side of that one."

"And you call me a pessimist? If you don't need me for anything right now—"

"I've got the sales lists you wanted to review for the weekend auction. I know you walked through the showrooms with Honey yesterday, but it wouldn't be a bad idea if we went through again with the sales lists in hand so you can match everything up and not be confused on auction night."

"I'll grant I was a little distracted by Honey, but I think I can still tell the difference between a bed and a highboy, thank you very much. Anyway, I can do that later. The auction is still two days away."

"The showrooms are already getting busy with bidders looking over the merchandise," Dylan warned. "And I don't think you want to be talking about target prices where buyers could possibly overhear."

"So I'll come in early tomorrow."

"Of course, if Mitchell signs a contract, you'll be up to your elbows in autographs by then."

"May I be so lucky," Amy murmured as if saying a prayer. "But that reminds me of what I started to tell you. If you don't need me for anything right now, I'm going downstairs to the library and bone up on autographs so I can sound as if I know what I'm talking about tonight."

"Are you certain you don't want me to come with you to see the collection? Two sets of eyes are better than one when it comes to catching details."

Amy shook her head. "If it looks worthwhile at all, I'll have to call in an expert anyway."

"Also, if Mitchell should be stubborn about making a deal, having two against one makes a lot better odds of convincing him."

"Not if he's feeling itchy about one of the two. I think

your time would be better spent in getting a phone number for an expert—someone who can evaluate not only autographs but the age of ink and paper, stuff like that. Then, if the collection does look promising, I can get an authoritative opinion right away.''

"I can run that down this afternoon."

Amy stared at him. "You mean you're not going to argue about whose job it is? And volunteering to come with me would mean you'd be working overtime two nights in a row... Dylan, are you certain you're not ill?"

She thought for a moment that he wasn't going to answer. "I've just got a feeling."

"About the autographs? I can handle it."

"Not the autographs exactly."

Amy stared at him for a moment. "All right," she said finally, "what is it between you and Mitchell Harlow? You seemed to be perfectly friendly yesterday morning in the Plaza."

"That was before he got a good look at you. I expected he'd be interested, but I didn't anticipate that he'd be stunned."

"Don't be silly, Dylan. He's got his mind on yachts and Lamborghinis."

"That line of his about you looking at the collection sounded an awfully lot like the villain murmuring, 'Wouldn't you like to come up and see my etchings?'" He gave a theatrical leer and twirled the end of an imaginary handlebar mustache.

"You're not seriously suggesting that the autographs are only an excuse to get me to his apartment," Amy said.

"Oh, I believe he's considering selling them. I just think he has other things on his mind, too."

The memory of the way Mitchell had pressed her hand

between his nagged at Amy for a moment. Was it possible Dylan was right?

She was already in the library, starting to pull reference books off the heavily loaded shelves, before she realized that Dylan had never really answered her question. *What is it between you and Mitchell Harlow?* she'd asked, and instead of answering he'd implied that Mitchell was attracted to her. But what exactly did that have to do with Dylan?

The apartment tower where Mitchell Harlow lived overlooked Country Club Plaza, making the sprawling shopping district a natural choice for his regular morning jogs. The building also had a reputation as the most expensive in Kansas City, and Mitchell's home near the top of the tower was one of the more desirable locations, probably second only to the Maxwells' penthouse.

No wonder Mitchell hadn't thought seriously before now about selling the autographs, Amy thought. Though his regular income might not run to floating pleasure palaces, he obviously didn't have any trouble making ends meet.

The security officer at the main door checked Amy's name off his list and phoned upstairs to confirm that she was on her way. While she waited, she couldn't help looking at the clipboard which held the very short list of visitors who were expected by tower residents that evening. It was lying on the desk at an awkward angle, so she couldn't have read all the names even if she'd been nosy enough to try. But she surely couldn't have missed seeing Dylan's name if it had been there, because it would have been right next to her own. Which it was not.

So she'd definitely read Mitchell correctly, and she'd

made the right choice in leaving Dylan out of this consultation.

What is it between you and Mitchell Harlow?

But she didn't have time to wonder about it, for the elevator silently and swiftly took her almost to the top of the tower. Mitchell was waiting in the lobby, the main door of the condo standing open behind him. He ushered her into an enormous living room where a wall of glass looked out over the Moorish-style buildings of Country Club Plaza and on to the skyline in the distance. She caught her breath at the vista.

Mitchell smiled indulgently. "It's pretty, isn't it?" He waved a hand at a squashy black leather sofa which was ideally placed to capture the view. "Would you like a glass of wine?"

"Later, perhaps," Amy said. "I wouldn't want to take a chance of spilling a drop on an important document."

"But my man has already opened the bottle. I thought perhaps we'd talk first and look at autographs later."

A tiny warning bell went off in the back of Amy's mind.

"I want to find out about auctions and things," Mitchell went on. "What you do all the time. I don't know much about how it all works." He filled a stemmed glass with red wine and handed it to her.

She relaxed, took the glass, and sat down on one end of the sofa, smiling inwardly at herself. How suggestible could a woman be, anyway? Just because Dylan thought he saw wolves lurking at the edge of the forest didn't mean they were really there—but one ambiguous comment from Mitchell and she had been ready to shriek and run. What had she been thinking? Mitchell Harlow was far from a wolf.

"Perhaps you'd like to come to the auction we're

holding on Friday evening,'' she said. ''The items we'll be auctioning are much different than your collection, of course, but the process is the same, and actually watching it happen will be much more enjoyable than listening to me try to explain it.''

He sampled his wine. ''You'll probably have to explain it to me anyway. But sure, if you want me to come, I'll be there.''

''I'll have a messenger deliver a ticket for you tomorrow.''

''It takes a special ticket?'' He sounded awed. ''Like a theater or something?''

''We don't charge admission, of course. But there's space in the auction rooms for only a couple of hundred people, so we try to make certain they're really interested in the merchandise, not just curious.''

Mitchell nodded wisely. ''Cheese and crackers?''

''No, thanks.'' Amy gestured toward a table almost covered with stacks of boxes. ''Is that the collection?''

He looked over his shoulder as if he wasn't sure what she was talking about. ''Yeah, that's it.''

Amy hadn't known what to expect. Scrapbooks, perhaps, with letters and documents mounted on each page—she'd just hoped that someone had known enough not to actually paste them in. She wouldn't even have been surprised to find Mitchell's much-lauded collection residing in a bureau drawer or a cardboard shoe box or a plastic crate.

But the display on the table startled her.

There must have been fifty boxes. None was very thick, and no two were quite alike; they varied in size from the kind of container that usually held engraved stationery to a large flat box that looked more like a map case. But they all matched, as if they'd been specially made for the collection. Whatever the items inside turned out to be, someone had taken great care and expense to preserve them.

Her fingertips itched. She set her wineglass down on a table next to the couch and reached for her purse, pulling out a pair of white cotton gloves. "If I may," she said.

"Want me to bring them over to you?"

Amy shook her head and walked across the room.

Mitchell followed closely. "I'll open all the boxes for you. I don't know why my uncle bothered with them, because those fasteners can be tricky."

"I'll look at one at a time." She picked up the top box, set it on the one corner of the table which wasn't already piled full, and looked it over before carefully turning the brass tabs that held the lid on.

Mitchell shook his head. "You've got more patience than I have," he said admiringly.

"Most of the damage to old things is done by careless, impatient handling. People get in a hurry to see if there's a treasure hidden inside, and sometimes they ruin it in the process." She pulled on her gloves and lifted the lid.

Inside the box was a sheet of tissue paper, and under it was what looked like a piece of parchment covered with spindly script. Beneath that was another sheet of tissue. The box held nothing else. No wonder the boxes were so flat, Amy thought, if each one held just one document, one autograph.

"Listen," Mitchell said briskly, "if you're going to take your time with these things, I might as well have my man order dinner for us. There's a restaurant downstairs that'll bring up whatever you want. Filet mignon, lobster..." He raised his voice. "Jenkins! Come here."

Amy hardly heard him, and she barely noticed the

soft-footed servant who came to the door. She shook her head absently. "Nothing for me, thanks."

If the signature on that parchment was genuine, she was thinking, Mitchell Harlow was sitting on a gold mine.

She opened the next box, and then the next. Unlike the first box, most contained several documents. There were never more than half a dozen, however, and each was carefully separated with tissue.

Though she didn't recognize every single signature, there were several which set her heart beating faster. She had no idea how much time had passed when the final box, the map-size case, was closed once more and back in its place.

She sat down again and stared out at the skyline. The lights on the Plaza far below were dimmer now, the stores closed and the shoppers gone.

"Well?" Mitchell said. He'd hovered over her the whole time she worked, so closely that sometimes she could hardly move, and now he sat down next to her on the couch, turned toward her with his arm stretched along the high back.

"I still can't believe you keep those things right here," she said. She reached for her wineglass and realized she was still wearing her cotton gloves. She stripped them off and tucked them back into her purse.

"In the hall closet."

She shuddered just a little.

"It's where my uncle kept them." Mitchell sounded a little defensive. "This was his place, till I inherited it."

It must not be the average hall closet, Amy thought. Since Mitchell's uncle had gone to the effort of placing each separate document in its own box to preserve it, surely he'd given thought to protecting the boxes, too, and made the closet into a sort of safe. The insight made her feel a little better. Still, she wouldn't breathe easily until every last box was under lock and key in a fireproof vault.

"What do you think?" Mitchell asked. He shifted anxiously on the couch.

"We'll need to have everything authenticated, of course. That will take an expert a little time, and he'll want to check the provenance of each individual document."

Mitchell looked bewildered.

"That means knowing as much as possible about the item—mainly how it ended up in your uncle's collection. When he bought it, and from whom. But also, if we can find out, we'd like to be able to tell the eventual buyer where the document came from originally and where it's been ever since it was created. Your uncle probably kept records of his collection."

His expression lifted a little. "There's a notebook still in the closet. Is that the kind of thing you mean?"

"Probably. I'll need to take that, too."

"Take it?"

"Along with the autographs. I'd like to move them over to the auction house, Mitchell. We've got vaults and safes to keep them secure, and the expert can look at them there without bothering you. I'll give you a receipt, of course, because everything is still your property until it actually goes onto the auction block. Once the expert has made his assessment we can decide whether it would be best to auction them as a group or individually."

If he was going to hedge about putting the collection

up for sale, Amy thought, he'd do it now. She tried not to hold her breath.

"How much?"

"What is the collection worth, do you mean?" Amy bit her lip. Her brain wouldn't work fast enough to answer—or perhaps the problem was that she couldn't multiply that high in her head. "I'd suggest you not actually buy the yacht or the Lamborghini just yet," she said, "but I think it's safe to start looking for the one you like best. One of each, in fact."

He seemed puzzled. "Then you think—"

"I can't make any guarantees, Mitchell. Even the expert won't be able to, because so many factors influence the final sale price. But—" She lifted her wineglass in a toast. "Here's to your new yacht. And the Lamborghini."

Mitchell's broad face creased into a wide smile. He leaned around her raised glass, put both hands on her shoulders, pulled her toward him and planted a kiss squarely on her lips.

Amy tried to pull back, but he'd put an arm around her and was holding her tightly. One of her arms was squashed in his embrace; the other held her wineglass. The only possible defense that presented itself to her was to dump the wine on him. But that would be a bit excessive, surely—his kiss couldn't have been anything more than awkward, misplaced, but well-meant gratitude.

"I knew from the first that we were meant for each other," he said, punctuating nearly every word with kisses across her cheek, her temple, her forehead. "We think alike. I knew it when you said if you had lots of money you'd buy a Lamborghini and a yacht, because those are exactly the things I've always wanted."

That wasn't what she'd said, of course. However, Amy could hardly confess that she'd named those two things not because she longed for them herself but because they were the sort of showy and superficial possessions she had suspected Mitchell would find attractive.

She'd guessed right about his hidden ambitions, and she'd accomplished exactly what she'd intended. She'd landed an auction even more important than she'd let herself dream of, one that might even startle her father with its scale.

Unfortunately for Amy, Dylan was right—and her victory had come with a problem attached. A five-foot-six, prematurely balding, slightly pudgy problem.

Now she had to find a way to gently discourage Mitchell from thinking she was his soul mate, without making him so angry that he'd put the autographs back in the dark hall closet and let them rot.

It was really too warm for a fire, but the old man always said he enjoyed watching the flames dance, and so, no matter what the weather, each evening found him sitting beside the fireplace. Dylan thought it was more likely that—though the old man would never have admitted it—his elderly bones found the warmth just as appealing as did the reddish-gold dog who was sprawled at his feet, sound asleep.

Almost morosely, Dylan swirled the contents of his snifter and took a sip.

The elderly man sitting in the wing chair across from him, wrapped in an old-fashioned smoking jacket tailored of dark red brocade, finally spoke. "What do you think of the brandy, my boy?"

"What? Oh, it's fine."

"That's odd," the old man murmured. "I mean, of course, that it's odd you didn't even notice I filled your snifter with vinegar instead."

Startled, Dylan smelled the fumes from his glass.

The old man burst out laughing. "No, Dylan, it's brandy. I was only checking to see if your mind was still on this planet. There's been some doubt of it all evening."

"I'm sorry."

"It's that girl, isn't it?"

"If by *that girl* you mean Gavin Sherwood's daughter—"

"Is there another woman in your life that I should know about?"

"Not at the moment, no."

The elderly man leaned back in his chair and studied Dylan.

Aware of the scrutiny but trying to ignore it, Dylan went back to watching the flames. He had been preoccupied all evening, no question about it, even though it was foolish of him to be worried about Amy. She must have learned long ago how to take care of herself.

Still...

Fool, he told himself. *You're a fool.*

He stood up. "I'm going out for a bit."

"To shake off the fidgets? Good idea, my boy."

The dog woke with a start and lumbered to her feet, shaking herself.

"Come on, Reggie," Dylan said. "Let's go for a walk."

It can't hurt to check, he thought. *Just to make sure.*

Amy got a hand free and planted it firmly against Mitchell's chest, holding him as far away as she could.

He stopped feathering kisses over her face and studied her with a frown.

"Sorry, Mitchell," she said, "but I make it a habit not to get personally involved with my clients."

He didn't release her. "But you came here," he pointed out.

"Because the collection was here."

"You said you'd be here anytime I wanted—like you were eager to see me." He sounded perplexed. "And you didn't bring Copeland, even when he said straight out that he wanted to come. When you told him you'd have to think about whether he should come, too, I thought you wanted to see me alone, just like I wanted to see you."

Amy wanted to swear. Now it was perfectly clear to her how it had happened. With her mind focused on the autograph collection, she had been blind to all the nuances which had been flying round the auction house that morning—Mitchell's invitation, the implications that could be drawn from her own comments, the way he'd made it clear he didn't want Dylan to come along. She felt like a fool for not seeing it before.

Or perhaps she *had* seen Mitchell's infatuation but simply refused to admit it existed because it had threatened to keep her away from her goal.

"You made it sound like you wanted to escape from him," Mitchell said plaintively, "but you needed to use business as an excuse."

Dylan had seen this coming, of course. If she'd only brought him with her...

"I'm sorry, Mitchell," she said as gently as she could. "I had no idea you felt that way."

She heard a buzz in the distance and caught a glimpse of the soft-footed servant walking down the hall. A moment later she heard the murmur of a familiar voice. "Is Mr. Harlow at home? That's fine, I'll show myself in."

A moment later Dylan was standing in the arched doorway. He looked perfectly relaxed and at ease.

Amy shot a warning look at him. If he said the wrong thing now, they could kiss the auction of Mitchell's autograph collection goodbye.

His gaze met hers, and his eyebrows raised just a fraction of an inch. "Sorry to be so late, darling," he murmured, "but you wouldn't believe the trouble I've had getting here."

CHAPTER SEVEN

AMY tried to be unobtrusive about releasing the breath she'd been holding. It could have been worse, she told herself. But she'd better not chance anything more; quick action was called for.

"I should think you'd feel a need to apologize, Dylan," she said, doing her best to sound like a starchy schoolmarm. "Rush hour can't still be going on. Where you could have been all this time..." She took advantage of Mitchell's slackened hold and stood up. "Luckily you've gotten here just in time to help me carry these boxes down to my car."

She quickly loaded Dylan up with a stack of boxes in each arm. By the time she was finished, he could hardly see over the pile. Fortunately, though the sheer number and varying sizes of the boxes made them awkward to handle, none was heavy. With luck, between the two of them, they could get out of the condo with the entire autograph collection in one trip.

Perhaps, she hoped, they could be gone before Mitchell got his voice back—before he could react in anger and refuse to let her take the collection after all. At the moment, he looked as if someone had hit him over the head with a skillet, but Amy didn't expect that to last long.

Of course, when Mitchell had a chance to think it all over, if he decided he didn't want to sell after all, she would do the ethical thing—she would promptly and personally return every single box and every last scrap of paper. She simply wanted to insure that he didn't make his decision in the heat of the moment, in irritation at her or at Dylan. And if she had physical possession of the autographs, he'd have no choice but to take a little time.

"I'll be in touch as soon as I have that expert opinion," she told him. She gathered up the remainder of the boxes as gracefully as she could. "Thank you for taking the entire evening so I could look at the autographs so carefully."

In her haste to get away, Amy almost tripped over Dylan's Irish setter, who had planted herself on the welcome mat with her tongue lolling. Dylan gave a low whistle, and Reggie trotted after them toward the elevator, dragging her leash.

"I see we're in a hurry," Dylan said as the elevator doors closed behind them. "Are we stealing these boxes? No, wait a minute. Maybe I don't want to know the answer to that question. It would make me an accomplice."

"We're not stealing anything."

"Then you're kidnapping them instead. There's something definitely fishy about this."

"There is not," she said defensively. "Mitchell agreed to the sale. I just didn't want to give him a chance to change his mind."

"Why would he change it? What did you do, slug him?"

She stared at him in indignation. "What are you talking about, what did *I* do? What on earth made you come storming in there like Superman?"

The elevator stopped on the ground floor, and as they crossed the lobby, the security guard touched the brim of his cap. "Good night, Ms. Sherwood. Mr. Copeland."

Amy automatically nodded an acknowledgment, but she wasn't really listening to the guard. "Why did you even show up, Dylan? And how did you get in? Your name wasn't on the visitors' list earlier."

"Chalk it up to my native charm."

"Oh, that's a laugh. It was silly to pretend that you were just running late, too. For all you knew, I'd told Mitchell you definitely weren't coming."

"I was in the neighborhood and thought I'd check on how you were doing."

"You expect me to believe that you were out for a run at this hour, dog and all, and just stopped by for a friendly chat?"

"No," he said easily, pushing the main door open with his shoulder, "but I thought Mitchell would believe it. He's not the brightest spotlight in town. Then when I walked in and saw the mess you'd gotten yourself into—"

"I was not in a mess."

Dylan snorted. "You were trying to hold off an octopus with one hand. That's my idea of a mess."

"I was doing just fine without your interference."

"You looked at me as if you were going under for the third time and I had the only life preserver in the state."

"That was a warning look, you idiot! I was trying to tell you not to do anything at all. You could have blown the whole deal, Dylan. You still may have—calling me *darling* like that."

"It was the most efficient way to make Mitchell back off."

"By making him think there's something going on between us?"

"So what? He was already half-convinced about that.

That's why he was warning me off this morning in your office.''

Amy frowned. "He was warning you off?"

"Well, he thought he was."

What is it between you and Mitchell Harlow? she had asked Dylan. No wonder he hadn't answered. He probably suspected she'd have taken the whole thing seriously. Maybe even allowed herself to believe that Mitchell must have had good reason for his suspicions and that Dylan *was* interested in her...

Poor Dylan, she thought. Was he honestly afraid that she'd believe that sort of nonsense? Even, possibly, fear that she would come chasing after him on the strength of Mitchell's beliefs? If so, she decided, it was past time to put a stop to that idea.

"It's too bad you didn't tell me about it right then," Amy said. "We could have had a good laugh at the mere idea of the two of you duking it out over me."

Dylan shot a look at her. "I'm telling you, Mitchell believed it. That's why..." He paused. "Where's your car?"

"Over there, in the lot. That's why *what?*"

"That's why when I walked in and found him making the moves on you, I thought the best way to handle it was to gently let him know that I have a prior claim."

"*Gently?* You were about as subtle as a wrecking ball."

"Hey, I could have grabbed him by the throat instead, or demanded that he explain himself. Or I could have just punched him in the nose without asking questions. Would you have liked those techniques better?"

Amy tried to picture Dylan with his hands around Mitchell's neck, shaking him like a terrier with a rat, simply because he'd dared to touch her. But she couldn't make the image come clear in her mind. Not because Dylan wasn't capable of that sort of ferocity, because she suspected he was. Any man would be, if he really cared about the woman in question, and if she was honestly in danger. But casual violence wasn't his style.

She mused, "Besides, you were looking out for yourself, weren't you? If you'd actually punched him because he was messing with your girl, it would be a little harder for you to back out of this fictitious claim that I belong to you."

"Absolutely, sweetheart," Dylan said cheerfully. "But the subtle approach worked nicely. I didn't really commit myself, I didn't embarrass Mitchell nearly as much as I could have, and I got your cute little rear out of trouble."

"I wasn't in trouble. How many times do I have to tell you—" She tried to dig her keys out of her purse and finally set her stack of boxes down on the roof of the car so she could open the trunk lid.

Dylan arranged his piles of boxes in the trunk so they wouldn't slide and retrieved hers as well. "You're surely not going to say you were enjoying that mauling."

"Well, his technique could stand some work. But I didn't need to be rescued. I am perfectly capable of dealing with Mitchell Harlow—or anybody else who comes along."

He stepped back from the car and looked down at her, his eyes narrowed. Every nerve in Amy's body shivered. She hadn't intended to issue a challenge, but he obviously thought she'd thrown down the gauntlet—and he looked as if he was thinking of picking it up. Then he snorted sarcastically. "You looked like you were doing great, all right."

She started to breathe again, slowly. It was crazy, of

course, to feel that she'd had a narrow escape. It was only her imagination which had made her think he was considering kissing her in order to prove a point. And she was glad she'd misread his mind. Very glad indeed.

"So how were you going to deal with him?" Dylan asked easily.

Amy bit her lip. "I'm not quite sure," she admitted.

He gave a hoot of laughter. "But you're annoyed at me because I got you out of there? With the autograph collection, and—I might add—without Mitchell losing face entirely?"

"You have no idea what you were tampering with, Dylan. He had decided to sell because he thought I wanted to share his yacht and his Lamborghini."

"Really? And when were you going to tell him you don't cherish those particular feelings about him, or his possessions?"

Amy plunged straight on. "Then you come bursting in announcing that I'm your personal property. You could have ruined everything."

He leaned against the side of her car, arms folded across his chest, and surveyed her. In the yellowish lights that illuminated the parking lot, his eyes were very dark. The crisp breeze ruffled his hair and made Amy shiver, but he didn't seem to notice the chill. At his feet, the dog whined.

"I think I see," Dylan said slowly. "You intended to just string the poor duck along till after you've auctioned his property. So that's why you didn't want me to scare him off. Tell me, Amy—just how far are you willing to go to get this auction?"

Amy was stunned. Was he really suggesting what it sounded like? "Not as far as you seem to think." She tried to push past him to get into her car.

Dylan stepped back and opened the door with a small, ironic bow. "But you'd obviously rather run away than discuss it. Okay—that's your right."

Amy was seething. He didn't need to make it sound as if she needed his permission to walk away from the discussion.

"See you tomorrow morning," Dylan said.

"Only because I don't have a choice," she muttered as she started the engine.

Amy swept past Dylan the next morning without a glance at him. A moment later he followed her into Gavin's office. She was still putting her handbag into the bottom desk drawer when he came in, and she didn't look up.

"You know, Dylan," she said, "I'm going to suggest to my father that the first thing he do when he comes back to work is to put a lock on that door. It would have saved a lot of trouble for him and for me. I'd have never walked in on him with Honey, you wouldn't be able to pop in and annoy me without invitation…"

"Point taken," Dylan said. "I came in to apologize."

Amy sat down in the big desk chair with an exaggerated thump and gave him a wide-eyed stare.

"You don't need to be sarcastic about it," he protested.

"I didn't say a word."

"You don't have to. Acid is oozing from every pore."

"Well, you must admit it's a surprise, you saying you're sorry. No, I get it now—you're obviously not apologizing for what happened last night. So you must have done something else entirely. Let's see—maybe you chipped my paperweight?" She picked up the pre-Columbian statuette from the desk and inspected it for damage. "No, it looks all right. You accidentally cut off an important phone call? Or maybe you just forgot to tell me something—"

In the same tone which had hushed the Battling Bensons, Dylan said, "I'm sorry for what I said last night."

Amy let the silence lengthen while she considered his words. "What you said?" she asked finally. "Not what you did?"

"I shouldn't have implied that you'd sleep with Mitchell if that was what it took to get the auction."

She shuffled papers on her desk. "And that's all?" she said calmly.

He braced both hands on the desk and leaned across it, his face close to hers. "Damn right that's all. If you're expecting me to apologize for coming up to Mitchell's apartment to pull your sorry little behind out of trouble—"

"Last night you said it was a cute little rear."

"A manner of speaking, that's all."

"What a relief. Because I'd hate to think you've been wasting your time watching whenever I walk across a room."

"I don't believe this. I try to apologize and you turn it into a personal attack."

"Apology accepted. Does that satisfy you? Now I have work to do."

Dylan didn't move. "I suppose you want me to clear out while you call Mitchell and set up another date."

Ostentatiously Amy pulled a folder from the top of the stack—yet another of Gavin's potential clients, one she hadn't looked at before—and opened it. But the words on the page in her father's neat handwriting swam before her eyes. "Of course," she snapped. "I'll obviously have to do it myself—because you're not a secretary.''

He released a long breath. ''I'm sorry, Amy. Again.''

She didn't look at him. She nodded and rubbed at the back of her neck, where her muscles had tightened into rigid bundles.

He moved around behind her chair and put his hands on her shoulders. Amy tensed, and Dylan murmured, ''I won't hurt you. Want to tell me about it?''

''No,'' she said. But he didn't seem to hear. With what appeared to be infinite patience, he rubbed her neck and shoulders, the warmth of his hands relaxing the tight muscles and his fingertips gently soothing away the tension.

''What is it, Amy?'' he said finally. ''Why is it so important to get this auction?''

She let the silence draw out.

''You don't have to prove yourself to your father. Gavin trusts you or he wouldn't have asked you to take over for him.''

''That's exactly why I have to do it. Because Gavin trusts me.'' A faint note of irony had crept into her voice.

It was apparent that Dylan heard it, for he paused for a moment before starting to massage again.

Amy surrendered. She closed her eyes and let her head droop forward, and she told him about Gavin's financial shortfall and the payment which was soon due to her mother in order to settle the last of the couple's financial entanglements.

Dylan gave a low whistle. ''I didn't know about that.''

''Of course you didn't. The last thing he wants is for it to be public knowledge that he's in financial trouble.''

Dylan's fingers stilled.

Amy sighed. "I didn't mean that the way it sounded. Of course you wouldn't announce it to the world. But he doesn't want anyone to think less of him." She patted the stack of folders. "He'd be calling everybody he knows and scrounging for business himself if he could. But since he can't—"

"You're out beating the bushes for a Picasso or an autograph collection to sell."

She craned her neck to glance up at him. "You sound surprised."

"Yeah," he said slowly. "At least, I'm surprised that you're so eager to help him be free that you're killing yourself to raise the money he needs."

Amy frowned. "How I feel about Honey doesn't have anything to do with it. Even if he can't make the payment on time, it won't stop the divorce from being final."

"Then why doesn't he just confess to Carol and ask for a delay?"

Amy looked at him in disbelief. "You've known my father for six months, and you're asking that? His pride, for one thing. Can you really imagine him admitting to his soon-to-be-ex-wife that he's pinched for cash?"

Dylan shook his head, but he said, "He dragged you into it quickly enough."

"Believe me, he didn't want to tell me. And he won't tell Mother because he's afraid she wouldn't agree to a delay."

"What do you think she'd do, if he asked?"

Amy thought about the talk she'd had with her mother just a couple of days ago, and how much Carol's lack of hostility had surprised her. "I don't know. She's got every right to be vindictive, though I don't think she would be. Still, I can't see her being very understanding, either, and I wouldn't blame her. If he can still find the money to take Honey to Italy but can't settle his obligations to Mother—"

"You've got a point there."

"And what's to say, if she lets him off the hook now, that he'll ever have the cash to pay her what he owes, with Honey in control of the finances? No, I made a promise to him and I'll stick to it. Whatever it takes."

Dylan gave a final rub to her shoulders and walked around the desk. "I'll go call Mitchell if you want."

Amy looked up at him, startled. "I was only joking about making another date."

"I know you were. But I could tell him that I overstepped my bounds last night and you've told me off royally."

"I'm not sure that would help. He'd probably think I did it to clear the way for him."

"He does have a pretty sizeable ego," Dylan agreed. "He might try again. But if I also confided in him that you made it plenty clear to me that nobody has a claim on you—"

The offer left Amy with an oddly hollow feeling.

"No, thanks," she said. "Leave Mitchell to me."

But the only thing Amy did about Mitchell Harlow was to call the expert Dylan had found. Until Mitchell told her differently, she decided, she would act as if the auction was going to happen—and that meant proceeding as she would with any other client. So once the expert had agreed, with barely repressed fervor, to drive up from Oklahoma City the next day to take a look at the collection, she did her best to put the matter out of her mind. Still, she couldn't help the little jolt of panic that ran through her veins every time her telephone rang, for fear that it might be Mitchell calling to demand his autographs be returned. Finally she tossed aside Gavin's notes about a woman who might consider parting with her Tiffany lamp and told Dylan she was going down to the showrooms to get ready for the following evening's auction.

A huge cart was almost blocking the doorway of the auction room, and a maintenance crew was already at work inside, setting up rows of small chairs for the bidders. They worked quickly and efficiently, despite the complexity of the pattern they were following.

At Sherwood's, there were no long straight rows of seats, no wide center aisle. Instead chairs were set at angles and in curves in an ornate arrangement that not only looked elegant, roomy and airy but left no seat far from an aisle.

Amy watched for a couple of minutes with a reminiscent smile. The pattern was her own, the product of a math class years ago. Challenged to apply geometric theory to practical use, she had figured out a way to put an extra fifty chairs in the room while making it look elegant rather than simply crowded. Her father hadn't believed she could do it, until he'd seen the room set up for the first time according to her instructions. Then he'd turned to stare at her with an expression she'd never seen before, and said something about her being a natural, a true Sherwood.

That sort of creative innovation was one of the things she had missed most about the auction business, Amy admitted. Seeing a problem and solving it, in an elegant sort of way, had been one of her greatest sources of enjoyment.

But there was no sense dwelling on regrets right now. She had a job to do, and as soon as it was done she'd be gone again. There was nothing else she could do, Amy knew. However much she missed the auction house, she could never come back full time. If her father hoped that this stint as manager would change her mind…

"Then he should have kept Honey under wraps," she muttered, and crossed the lobby to the showrooms to begin painstakingly matching each item against its catalog description.

It was probably needless homework, she realized, because both the catalog and the sales list Dylan had given her were clear, well-organized, and specific. Nevertheless, she knew she'd feel more confident at the podium on Friday evening if she knew every detail about each piece, its source and history and the price it was expected to bring.

And, she reflected, it helped keep her mind off Mitchell Harlow and the autographs.

She was halfway through the main showroom, mentally cataloguing and appraising each item before checking the list, when Dylan came in. Hanging on his arm was a tall, slim blonde who gasped at the sight of the Chippendale highboy just inside the showroom—the same one that had made Honey wrinkle her nose at the idea of ancient dust. "Oh, Dylan—it's so beautiful!" she cried.

Her voice sliced through the Bach concerto on the sound system and grated on Amy's nerves. The single other visitor in the quiet showroom looked at the woman with ill-concealed distaste for her disruption. His escort, one of Beth Gleason's china appraisers, murmured something in a low voice and pointed at the next piece of furniture.

Amy glanced at it too, and recited mentally, *Regency*

rosewood and parcel-gilt center table with inlaid marble panel. Valued at...

"There you are, Amy," Dylan said. "I'd like to introduce Sarah Harkness."

Amy shifted the sales list to her other arm and held out a hand. "Are you a collector, Ms. Harness?"

"Only in a small way." Sarah Harkness took one hand off Dylan's arm just long enough to limply shake Amy's. "Though of course I wish I could afford a piece or two like this." She was looking at the highboy, but her fingers were running lightly along Dylan's coat sleeve.

Are we talking about furniture or masculinity? Amy wanted to ask.

"Robert's looking for you, Amy," Dylan said.

Amy's heart jolted. Was this the call she'd been waiting for all morning, while hoping it wouldn't come? "Mitchell Harlow?"

"No," he said. "Sorry, I didn't even think about that. Your mother's down in the reception area. I offered to bring her upstairs, but she said she'd wait till she knew you were still in the building."

Amy frowned. "Mother? I wonder what brings her here." But of course, Carol knew that since Gavin was nowhere around, it would be quite safe for her to drop by. "I'll go see what she wants."

Dylan looked across her toward the lobby. "You don't need to," he said dryly.

Carol Sherwood had paused just outside the showroom. "I changed my mind," she said, "and decided to come up after all. I know it's against the rules, but don't blame Robert, Amy. We both thought I could catch up with Dylan before he got out of the lower lobby."

Amy went to greet her mother. "Easier said than

done,'' she murmured, her gaze once more on Sarah Harkness's hands, which were now clasped tightly around Dylan's arm. ''He—and his guests—move fast.''

Carol kissed her cheek. ''Hello, dear.''

''What's going on, Mom? Are you taking me up on that invitation to lunch a couple of days ago?'' Amy tried to keep her tone light.

''I've got myself in a bind, I'm afraid,'' Carol said.

''Let's go up to my office.''

Slowly Carol shook her head. ''I'd rather not, Amy. It's one thing for me to be here, in the areas that are open to the public—even though I've never been required to have an escort to come into the showrooms before.'' She sounded just a little bitter. ''I completely understand, of course, and I know it's not your doing, it's Gavin's. But I wouldn't feel at all comfortable upstairs in your father's office.''

''Oh.'' Amy felt like a fool. ''Of course you wouldn't. I'm sorry.'' She drew her mother a bit away from the others. ''What can I do for you?''

Carol sighed. ''It's nothing earthshaking, really. It's just this silly sorority I belong to. You know they fund a couple of scholarships for women over at the college.''

Amy nodded.

''Well, the members took a notion this year to have an auction, and I must say they've collected some very interesting items to sell.''

''And they've asked you to find an auctioneer?'' Amy was relieved. Of all the things Carol could be asking for, that was among the easiest to provide. Almost giddy with relief, and feeling ever so slightly malicious, she raised her voice a trifle. ''I'll send Dylan. It'll give him some good practice.''

He was standing almost halfway down the length of

the showroom with Sarah Harkness still dangling from his arm, but Amy didn't miss the quick turn of his head when he heard his name. The look he gave her made her want to giggle.

She turned back to Carol. "When is the auction, Mother?"

"Saturday evening."

Amy's jaw dropped. "You mean this weekend? Left it a little late, didn't they?"

"Not really, dear. When the idea first came up, of course everyone thought Gavin would…" Carol's voice trailed off. "Anyway, they found someone else, but at the last minute he's canceled and they asked in desperation if I could do something."

Amy rubbed the bridge of her nose. "Sure. I'll do it."

"I knew I could count on you, dear. And you're quite right about it being good practice for Dylan. Wait till I tell the girls who I've got."

"Actually I was joking about Dylan," Amy began.

He spoke from behind her. "I'd be happy to lend Amy a hand, Carol. Otherwise she'll have back-to-back auctions."

"Thanks," Amy said irritably, "but selling a bunch of donated merchandise would hardly present the same sort of pressure that all this furniture will."

"You might be surprised, honey." Carol's voice was dry. "A bunch of amateurs are always harder to deal with than people who are experienced. Just to thank you both, I'll take you out for dinner before—"

From the other end of the showroom came a high-pitched squeal. "Oh, look," Sarah Harkness cried. "That bed—isn't it simply wonderful?"

Amy felt her heart drop. She hadn't gotten that far in her tour, and she hadn't given a thought all morning to the bed. The Georgian bed that had belonged to Gavin and Carol.

She found herself watching not Carol but Dylan—and seeing her own consternation reflected in his eyes. They were obviously thinking precisely the same thing: Did Carol know that Gavin had put their bed up for sale?

Slowly, almost in unison, they turned to look at Carol.

She had taken a step forward, and she was standing in the middle of a beam of light from a spotlight which should have been focused on the intricately inlaid top of a marquetry desk. Her head was held high, and the tears which filled her eyes and gleamed in the spotlight did not overflow.

Amy, lost for words, took refuge in making a mental note to tell the maintenance crew to readjust the spotlight to its proper position.

Carol swallowed hard. "So that's why he wanted it," she said levelly. "He spun me a tale about how much sentimental value it had for him. And I was fool enough to believe it. I wonder what he'll say about it now."

Before Amy could find her voice, Carol marched across the showroom and out into the lobby.

Amy dropped the sale list and followed her. She had no idea how she was going to tell her mother that it had been Honey who insisted on selling the bed, but she knew she had to try.

Except, by the time Amy reached the top of the wide stairway, the door to the reception room was closing behind Carol, and it was too late.

CHAPTER EIGHT

IT TOOK Dylan an instant longer to react—perhaps, he thought, because he didn't know Carol as well as he'd thought he did. In all his dealings with her, Carol had maintained a habitual calm, and so he'd been slower than Amy to recognize the fury that had underlain her mother's voice.

He caught up with Amy at the top of the stairs, his hand closing on her arm just as she started down.. "Don't interfere," he urged.

She tried to shake him off. "Let me go! She's my mother, and it's none of your business."

"She's an adult." Half-afraid that if she managed to break free, she'd lose her balance and tumble down the stairs, Dylan tightened his grip. "She doesn't need your assistance."

"But she's going to confront Gavin."

"Maybe she will. Maybe she won't. But whatever happens now, it's between them. It doesn't involve you."

"But he's been ill. If she goes storming into his hospital room screaming at him—"

Dylan was honestly puzzled. "Why are you so afraid of what she'll do? That kind of behavior doesn't sound like the Carol I know."

She stopped struggling, as if to consider the question, and he drew her a few steps away from the top of the stairs. But he still didn't let go.

"You know her better than I do, of course," Dylan

said. "But she strikes me as the sort who could cut you to ribbons without ever raising her voice."

Amy tried to pry his fingers off her arm. "You're right, she's never been a screamer. Of course, the result is pretty much the same. If she goes to see him—"

"Do you really think you can stop her? You might keep her from going today, but you can't prevent her from seeing Gavin some other time, or calling him. Maybe it's better if she gets this out of her system while he's still in the hospital, Amy. If whatever she says to him raises his blood pressure an iota, the nurses will throw her out."

At last, he thought, he was getting through to her. He let go of her arm.

"Whatever happens," she said, "it's going to be awful."

"Maybe. But neither of them would thank you for getting in the middle."

She looked up at him with exasperation in her eyes. "And what exactly would you know about it?"

"Quite a lot, actually," Dylan said, almost under his breath.

Amy tipped her head to one side and studied him as if he were a new species.

Instantly he regretted giving in to the impulse to speak. He had expected that she'd be too absorbed in her own concerns to really hear him, or to realize that he wasn't thinking only of her parents.

She said, with a note of certainty, "And you learned it the hard way."

Dylan nodded. "Yes, I did. But this isn't a good time to go into the details. Or have you forgotten I left a client in the showroom, against all of Gavin's rules?"

She glanced vaguely toward the showroom, and

seemed to pull herself back from a distance. "Don't expect me to fire you over it," she said. "I think I dropped the sales list on the floor, where anyone could pick it up." She turned toward the showroom, but she was looking over her shoulder, as if hoping that her mother would think better of that stormy exit and reappear.

But at least, he thought, Amy wasn't going after her.

The sales list was still right where she'd dropped it. But the clip holding the pages together had slipped off in the fall, and it took Amy a couple of minutes to gather up all the sheets and get them back in order.

By then Dylan had rejoined Sarah Harkness, who was still standing beside the George III bed, admiring its size and luxury. Amy could hear part of the conversation—or, more accurately, she could hear Sarah's self-conscious giggles and deduce what she was saying. Irritated, she moved toward the far end of the showroom and forced herself to concentrate on the furniture. In little more than twenty-four hours the auction would start, she reminded herself, and she had to be ready.

There was a slow but constant stream of visitors looking over the furniture. Amy recognized a few dealers and a fair number of regular auction customers, but she also noted some brand-new faces. Of course, she hadn't been hanging around the showrooms for several months, so maybe they were new only to her.

Some of the lookers were obviously interested only in a particular piece and their visits were short. Others seemed to want to inspect everything, as if this was a kind of museum—one without ropes to bar visitors from touching the displays.

Sarah Harkness was one of the second sort, Amy thought. She apparently intended to check out each peg or nail, open every drawer, and trace every inlay. A casual onlooker would probably assume, from the intensity of her study, that she was an expert.

Except, Amy thought uncharitably, the woman would probably have displayed the same level of interest if she'd been looking at baseball cards, or muzzle-loaders, or stained-glass windows saved from a demolished church. She'd look just as long as Dylan stood patiently beside her.

But finally even Sarah Harkness had seen enough, and Dylan took her back to the reception area. Amy was relieved; the woman's high-pitched giggle had been rubbing her nerves.

She studied a Federal-style walnut breakfront bookcase and wondered if Carol had gone straight to the hospital. If so, the shouting could all be over by now.

Or maybe her mother had gotten thoroughly stuck in a traffic jam and had a chance to cool off, and she'd changed her mind.

It doesn't involve you, Dylan had said. Easy for him to say. Though obviously he had some firsthand experience along the way. She wondered where he'd gotten it, and only then realized how little she really knew about Dylan Copeland.

She paused beside the George III bed, fingertips stroking the heavy satin hangings. Lost in memory, she didn't hear Dylan come up beside her until he spoke.

"Still mad at me?"

Amy shook her head. She gave a last caress to the cream-colored satin. "This piece of furniture represents all that was best about their marriage. It's no wonder Mother lost control when she saw it here."

"That scene wasn't really about the bed, you know."

"What do you mean?"

"It was overdue. I've thought for quite a while that Carol was too calm about the whole thing."

Too calm? Amy remembered how surprised she had been at her mother's lack of anger. *Being vindictive is a waste of energy,* Carol had told her.

She shook her head. "All I can say is that she's a better actress than I realized she was."

"I don't think she was faking it. I'd guess she didn't even realize she was doing it."

"Repressing her anger, you mean?"

Dylan nodded. "Stuffing it so far down inside that even she thought she wasn't angry any more. It seems safer that way sometimes. The trouble is, it's hard to keep the genie in the bottle forever, because sooner or later something disturbs the cork."

"In this case," Amy mused, "seeing the bed where she least expected it."

"And when that happens there's an explosion. Bigger and worse than if it had happened in the natural course of events."

"That's exactly why I think I should have tried to stop her. Made her think about it, at any rate, before she went off like a stick of dynamite."

"On the other hand, maybe it's time that Gavin has to face the consequences of his actions," Dylan said softly.

Amy frowned. "I'm not sure I understand. Surely he—"

"All the way through this, Gavin's been able to convince himself that what he did really didn't hurt anybody but himself. He's the only one feeling the financial pinch. He's the one who lost the best assistant he could ever hope for."

"You mean me? You can't be serious that he thinks all this uproar hasn't affected me."

"Didn't you tell him how you were looking forward to all the wonderful new opportunities you have at the museum, the college, the magazine?"

"Yes," Amy said impatiently, "but... Oh. I see what you mean. If I ended up happier in my new job than I was here..."

"Then he had actually done you a favor—in a round-about and unintentional way, of course. As for your mother, Carol's been so understanding about the whole thing that it almost appeared she was happy to be out of the marriage."

That's what was bothering me, Amy realized. When Carol had told her how the Sherwoods had grown apart, when she'd refused to put the blame for the breakup on Gavin's infidelity.... *I thought she was relieved to be free.*

"It wouldn't have changed anything if she'd screamed and yelled," Amy said. "At least this way she kept her dignity." She faced him. "So how do you know all this? Personal experience, obviously."

Dylan nodded. "My parents split when I was ten. I did all the classic things—blaming myself, acting up, pulling every stunt in the book to get them back together, trying to keep them from hurting each other."

His parents. It hadn't been his own marriage, then. She was glad of that, for his sake, because the pain of divorce was bad enough even secondhand. And perhaps that explained why he didn't seem to want to get involved.

Don't kid yourself, she thought. Just because he obviously hadn't wanted to get involved with Amy didn't mean he couldn't be interested in someone else.

"None of it made any difference, of course," Dylan said. "It never does. They have to work it out between themselves. Putting yourself between them would only make you a target. If you're finished here, Amy, Beth Gleason wants to talk to you. She was just coming in when I took Sarah downstairs."

"I thought she was inventorying at the Benson house today."

"She tried, but what she calls the three weird sisters kept interfering."

Amy frowned. "But they agreed to the plan. Why would they want to keep her from working?"

"Oh, they weren't trying to stop the inventory. They said they were just observing to be sure nothing was overlooked."

"I'll bet. I'm surprised they were so tactful. I'd expect them to come right out and say they thought she was going to steal anything they might not miss. You should have given me that advice about not getting in the middle just a little earlier, Dylan—before I was fool enough to take on the Battling Bensons. How far did Beth get with the inventory?"

"She said she got through the display case in the main hallway and the coat closet by the front door."

"At that rate we'll have the whole staff tied up for weeks." Amy sighed. "I don't see what we can do, short of calling the whole thing off."

"I think we need to go over in the morning and talk to them."

"We?"

"Well, I feel some obligation to Bill to follow through. And the family auction was your idea in the first place."

"Please don't remind me."

"Besides, once you're back in that atmosphere, maybe you'll come up with another inspiration."

"That," Amy said, "is exactly what I'm afraid of."

Dylan was right, Amy knew. She couldn't hope to heal the breach between her parents, and if she tried to act as a buffer between them, both Gavin and Carol were more likely to think she was interfering than helping. The effort would make her a handy object of irritation for both of them and perhaps make it even harder for them to reach any resolution.

"Who has time to play peacemaker, anyway?" she muttered. She'd spent twelve straight hours at the auction house today, and tomorrow—with the auction in the evening—would no doubt be even longer.

Still, though she hadn't consciously decided to go to the hospital, Amy found herself in the parking ramp just outside. She wouldn't try to intervene, she told herself, or to cover up any wounds. But she had to see for herself if there had been any more damage done.

Gavin was sitting up in bed, and he looked much better than he had a few days before, when Amy had last seen him. There was less machinery surrounding him, and he had much more color. Though—on second thought—she wasn't sure if the red in his cheeks was a sign of improved health or just plain anger.

She was in the room before she realized that a nurse was at his bedside. "Sorry," she said quickly. "I'll wait outside."

The nurse shook her head. "I'm almost finished. Just a routine check of vital signs."

Amy leaned on the rail on the opposite side of the bed. A copy of the new issue of *Connoisseur's Choice* lay on Gavin's lap, open to the column which reported the most notable recent auction prices. That was a good sign, Amy thought. He was taking every means to keep himself up-to-date. On the other hand, the magazine might be an attempt to distract himself from thinking.

"I thought they were going to let you go home by now." *Unless you've had a setback.*

The nurse took off her stethoscope and bundled the blood pressure cuff back into its holder. "Oh, we've gotten so fond of him around here we don't want to let him go."

Which tells me exactly nothing.

Gavin tapped the magazine page. "So this is where you think you want to work."

"I'm sure I'd like the job."

Gavin surveyed her, eyes narrowed. "Roving expert," he said. "Not much different than what you're doing right now, you know."

Except for small things like Mitchell Harlow and the Battling Bensons.... "I don't know about the expert part," Amy said wryly. "I'm certainly doing the roving."

"How's it going?"

"I've got an authority coming in tomorrow to look at Mitchell Harlow's autograph collection."

Gavin beamed. "That's my girl."

"Don't celebrate just yet. I haven't got the most important signature of all yet—his name on a sales contract."

"You'll get it," Gavin said.

"I hope you're right, because time's getting short." She looked straight at him and added deliberately, "And Mother wants to take a trip around the world, or something equally grand, as soon as she gets her money." Surely, she thought, if Carol had come to see him today, if there had been a conflict, that would push Gavin into admitting it. He would have to tell her—wouldn't he?

He didn't react for a long moment. "I see," Gavin murmured. "I see."

But that was all he said.

The Bensons—as Amy still thought of them, despite their differing last names—had gathered just as she had requested in the dining room of the Ward Parkway mansion. They were prompt, which was more than Amy had expected. All four of them were already on hand when she and Dylan arrived.

But any faint hope she had nourished that getting them into the same room would inspire them to talk to each other died the moment Amy came in. Two of the sisters were pacing the floor, at right angles to each other so they never made eye contact. Hattie, who'd been part of the initial squabble, was standing in front of the china cabinet; her lips were moving as if she were counting pieces. Only Bill Benson, already seated at the table, appeared at first glance to be at ease, but his too-casual pose gave him away.

One of the sisters stopped pacing when they came in. She raked a glance over Amy and Dylan and said, "And what do you know about valuable antiques, anyway? You're far too young."

"Do you really think one has to be an antique to appreciate one?" Amy asked pleasantly.

"Well, I never!" the woman said. "Hardly in the door and she insults me."

"Can't say you didn't ask for it," Hattie observed.

Amy had to think about it before she could even find the perceived insult. "I suppose you could assume I was saying that you're old, though that's not what I meant.

Or you could look at it the other way, and conclude that I'm complimenting your good taste and knowledge.''

The woman sniffed.

Amy said, ''I've called this meeting because our staff feels their work is being constrained by constant observation.''

''They're being paid,'' the other sister put in.

''By the hour,'' Amy pointed out. ''The more quickly they can do the job, the more money will be left for you four.'' *To fight over.* ''I have two choices. I can either put so many people on the job that you can't possibly follow them all. Or, if the interference continues, I can pull them off the job entirely and leave you to settle your differences between yourselves.''

There were mutters, but no protests, and though they grumbled, the four agreed to allow the crew to work without hindrance.

''Let them work and this will soon be settled,'' Amy reminded. ''And once it's over you won't even have to see each other again.''

''Congratulations,'' Dylan said on the way back to the auction house.

''What do you mean, congratulations?''

''For getting an agreement out of the Fearsome Foursome.''

''I consider that a spectacular failure,'' Amy muttered. ''I was hoping they'd fire us.''

There was always tension in the air on the day of an auction, an almost palpable excitement that ran through the whole building. Everyone involved in the process felt it, from the clients taking a last-minute look at the merchandise to the maintenance workers who were on hand to shift merchandise from showroom to auction room.

And though there was never a truly quiet time in the building, it was most alive on auction nights, full of bright lights and music and the sparkle of guests in their dress-up best.

Amy stood at the foot of the stairs so she could greet the guests as soon as they'd presented their tickets to the curators who waited at the door. Some stopped to chat with her for a moment or to ask about Gavin, but most just smiled and moved on up the stairs to the auction room to take their seats.

After the first wave of guests had gone upstairs, Dylan came down from the auction room, where he'd been helping people find their seats. Amy had seen him wearing a tuxedo before, at previous auctions. But tonight, she thought, he looked particularly distinguished.

Perhaps it was the fact that with Gavin absent, he wasn't standing in the older man's shadow. For years Gavin had been the personification of the auction company, and when he was around, he was always at center stage.

Not that Dylan could ever be overlooked, Amy thought. He was hardly what she'd call self-effacing. On the other hand, he never pushed himself forward, either, just as tonight he had volunteered to watch from behind the scenes so Amy didn't have to concern herself with details.

She wondered why he seemed to prefer to stay out of the public eye. No, that wasn't quite the right way to put it, either, she reflected, for he didn't avoid dealing with customers. He had thrust himself right into the case of the Battling Bensons.

And of course not everyone was the sort of showman and performer that Gavin was. Maybe it wasn't anything about Dylan at all, only the contrast between him and her father, which had struck her so sharply.

"Nervous?" Dylan asked.

Amy shook her head. "No, though I expected this would be the worst case of auction-night nerves I've ever had. I thought it would be worse even than the night my father handed me the gavel for the first time."

"How old were you?"

"About sixteen. And he didn't give me any warning."

"No wonder you were nervous."

She noticed that his emerald tie and cummerbund had added a green tint to his eyes, turning them almost teal instead of their normal blue. Or did they just appear darker than usual because he was looking at her so intensely? "Once I started, I forgot to be anxious. I loved it—he had to pry the gavel out of my hand."

Dylan said slowly, "You really love this business, don't you?"

Amy nodded.

"Then maybe you shouldn't leave. It is your legacy, after all."

"There won't be much of a legacy by the time Honey gets finished with it." Another group of customers came through the door, and she turned to greet them with a smile.

The first of them was Dylan's pal, Sarah Harkness. She was dressed as if she was going to a formal dance, in a low-cut silver-spangled gown, and she was even more giddy than she had been in the showroom yesterday. Her gaze slid carelessly over Amy and focused on Dylan. "I'm so excited," she said in a husky whisper. "I just can't believe I'm really here."

Dylan offered the woman his arm. "I'll take Sarah upstairs to her seat, Amy."

Please do, Amy thought. *Because if I have to listen to her giggle once more, I won't be responsible for what I do.* "I hope you'll enjoy the evening, Ms. Harkness," she said and looked past her to the next guest—one she hadn't seen since the night of the Maxwells' cocktail party. "Brad," she said in surprise. "I knew *Connoisseur's Choice* publishes auction prices, but I didn't expect you'd be covering the event yourself."

Brad Parker gave a sniff. "It's not on my usual beat. Amy, this is Eric Dougal, the magazine's publisher."

Amy's heart beat a little faster as she looked at the man standing beside him. Eric Dougal had been a tall man, but now he was slightly stooped with age; his hair gleamed almost silver in the soft light which filled the lobby. Amy had seen photos of him, but she'd never met him before. Though Eric Dougal was a legend in the world of antiques, in the past few years he was seldom seen in public. So why was he here tonight?

Eric Dougal shifted his silver-topped walking stick so he could take Amy's outstretched hand. "So you're the young woman who's keeping Brad on hold," he said. His voice was warm and rich, with an undertone of humor.

Amy was taken aback. She had guessed, from the tone of Brad's voice, that it hadn't been his choice to attend the auction—but it hardly seemed likely that Eric Dougal would be interested enough in a possible future employee to make this kind of effort.

"Only because my father needed me to fill in just now, sir," she said quietly.

Eric Dougal glanced around the crowded lobby. "Obviously," he murmured. "I understand you have some very interesting pieces to sell tonight, Ms. Sherwood."

"I don't think you'll be disappointed, sir. If you'd like

a catalog, they're just outside the auction room. Let me get someone who can find you a good seat.''

She looked around, trying not to appear desperate. Why couldn't Dylan have stuck around just one minute longer, she thought irritably, so he could have made certain that Eric Dougal got the best seat in the house? Of course, a few minutes ago she'd been grateful that Dylan had removed Sarah Harkness from the lobby...

Eric Dougal's eyes twinkled. ''I'm sure we can manage,'' he murmured, and he and Brad started up the stairs.

In the few moments she'd been concentrating on Eric Dougal, a number of people had bypassed her and gone up the stairs or to the elevators. Honey was among them, she saw, and was grateful not to have to make small talk with her future stepmother in public.

Running her gaze across the crowd, she noticed abruptly that in the same group with Honey, waiting for one of the elevators, was Mitchell Harlow. Relief surged through her. She hadn't heard from him since she and Dylan had left his apartment with the autograph collection, and she wouldn't have bet a cent on whether he'd actually use the ticket she'd sent over the next day. But he'd come, and surely that was promising.

The crowd was only a trickle now, and it was almost time for the auction to begin. But the one person Amy had almost expected to attend—her mother—had not appeared.

What Carol would have done about the bed if she'd come to the auction, Amy didn't know. But she wouldn't have been surprised if Carol had wanted to see for herself what happened to it—to bring some closure to the episode, if nothing else.

Amy climbed the stairs and stood for a moment in the

doorway. Honey, of course, had found a seat right at the front of the room, only a few chairs down from Sarah Harkness, who had perhaps the best seat in the house. *What a surprise,* Amy thought irritably. Just one row behind them, in an aisle seat, was Mitchell Harlow.

It took Amy a minute to locate Eric Dougal, who was sitting almost at the back. She caught Dylan's eye and waved him over. "The elderly gentleman in the back," she said shortly. "He should be sitting right up front."

Dylan followed her glance. "The white-haired one? It would be a little obvious to move him right now."

He was right. "At intermission, then." Amy walked across to the podium. The room hushed, falling so quiet that she could hear as well as feel the swish of her black silk skirt against her ankles. "Good evening, and welcome to Sherwood's," she said, and picked up the gavel. "Our first item is a Queen Anne walnut bachelor's chest, pictured on page ten of the catalog…"

Time seemed to slow as she dropped into the rhythm of the sale. Announce the item and read the full description so no one could possibly bid in error on an item they didn't want to buy. Pause for an instant to let the room come to attention. Ask for a bid at starting price. Watch not only the entire room but the phone bank along the far wall, where Beth Gleason and several other employees were relaying the action to bidders who couldn't attend in person. Keep the pace moving so the excitement built. Let the last bid hang for a moment so a hesitant bidder had time for second thoughts, and…

"Sold, to Mr. Kyle Emerson," Amy said. "The next item…"

I have missed this, she thought. *I hadn't even let myself realize how much.*

Sarah Harkness sat bolt upright, eyes wide, looking as

if she was afraid of missing something if she blinked. Honey sat almost sideways, legs crossed, doodling in her catalog. *Keeping track of Gavin's commissions,* Amy thought.

Mitchell was staring past the podium as if he was looking into next year instead of paying attention to the sale. And way in the back of the room, Eric Dougal looked around with mild amusement, seemingly more interested in observing people than furniture.

Amy lost track of time, but she could judge the progress of the auction by the catalogs lying open on bidders' laps. They were almost halfway when, the moment she accepted a final bid on the Italian mirror that Honey had so despised, Dylan appeared beside her and cupped a hand over the microphone. "The bed is coming up next," he said softly. "If you want, I'll go get someone to take over for you. You don't have to sell it yourself."

Amy choked up. It was thoughtful of him, to understand how difficult it would be for her to let the gavel fall on the George III bed that had meant so much to her and to her parents. But she shook her head. "I need to do this myself," she said.

He looked at her for a long moment, his eyes full of compassion. Then he nodded and moved a few feet off to one side. He could help spot bidders in the crowd, but he was still close enough that Amy could feel his strength backing her up.

Amy cleared her throat. "Our next item is a George III painted parcel-gilt four-poster bed…" Her voice was huskier than usual, she knew.

The bidding started slowly, seesawing between a couple of dealers. But as the price rose, the dealers dropped out and the serious collectors took over. Amy concentrated on the price and tried not to watch the faces.

Maybe Dylan had been right, she thought. If she'd excused herself—given the gavel to Beth Gleason—she wouldn't even have to know for sure who had purchased the bed.

The bidding ebbed, but suddenly Sarah Harkness held up her numbered paddle, agreeing to the price Amy was asking. Amy almost dropped her gavel.

The woman had left the impression yesterday that she didn't have the funds to be a serious buyer, but here she was bidding on one of the premiere items in the sale. Did Sarah know what she was doing, or had she suffered a sudden attack of auction fever? It happened sometimes—people got caught up in the excitement and bid madly, feverishly, and foolishly.

She glanced at Dylan, who gave a tiny shrug. Amy took the bid and went on.

To her relief, however, Sarah Harkness soon dropped out of the running. The two remaining bidders sparred for a while, then one shook his head and the other looked triumphant. "The bid is at thirty-four thousand," Amy said. "Do I hear another? Going—" Her voice caught and she had to stop for a moment. *This should never have happened,* she thought fiercely. But it was out of her hands now; she had to carry through and finish the job.

Breaking the silence, a low, rich voice from the back of the room said, "Forty."

The crowd, almost as one, craned to see who had spoken.

Amy's voice was ragged. "The bid is at forty thousand," she managed to say. "Going…going…sold to Mr. Eric Dougal."

Normally Amy spent the intermission among the clients, but tonight her only thought was to escape the clamor of the auction room to find some silence. She slipped away and climbed the stairs to her office. She didn't even turn on the lights, just stood in the middle of the room, hands clenched tight. *It's over,* she told herself. Now perhaps, with the symbol of her parents' marriage gone, she could truly accept the fact that the marriage itself was dead.

"That was very brave," Dylan said.

Amy wheeled around and saw him leaning against the doorjamb, watching her. She shook her head and tried to speak, but all that came out was a pathetic-sounding sob.

She didn't see him move, but an instant later he was beside her, and without considering what she was doing, she turned to him, nestling into his arms.

He held her close, his cheek against her hair. She didn't cry, she simply relaxed against him and let herself be comforted by his warmth—both physical and emotional.

Being in his arms was like floating, safe and secure. But after a moment Amy found herself wanting more— and feeling reckless enough to take the risk that accompanied the desire.

All she wanted was a kiss. A gesture of comfort, she would have said. Surely that wasn't asking too much.

She tipped her head back and looked up at him, and let the tip of her tongue run slowly along her lips. And he seemed to understand exactly what she wanted, for he kissed her slowly and gently.

Only it wasn't comforting at all. The kiss that should have soothed her soul set her aflame instead, despite his gentleness. The heat of her body seemed to leap to his.

He held her closer, and suddenly his kiss was neither slow nor gentle, but hot and fierce and demanding.

This, Amy thought, *is the way it should be. The way I want it to be for always.*

And a small voice in the back of her brain asked, *How long do you suppose you've loved him?*

CHAPTER NINE

THE question was almost casual, so natural that it was a
moment before Amy even realized what she was thinking. But when it finally did register, she felt as if she
was caught in a slow-motion earthquake.

I can't have fallen in love with him, she thought fran-
tically. She couldn't possibly have done anything so stupid.

For there was no question that allowing herself to become emotionally embroiled with him *was* stupid. It
wasn't as if Dylan had encouraged her, or singled her
out to make her feel special. Far from it, in fact. He'd
always been friendly enough to her—but he was equally
friendly to everybody else.

When he'd first come to work for Gavin, Amy had
been attracted to him. There was no sense in denying it,
because any woman with average eyesight and ordinary
instincts would have been drawn to him. And, being a
normal woman, she had acted on that attraction. She'd
flirted just a little. She'd created occasions to go up to
the executive offices. She'd taken advantage of opportunities to stop and chat. But it had been nothing more
than that—whatever Beth Gleason wanted to think, Amy
hadn't thrown herself at Dylan. She had only tossed a
few hints.

Hints which he had simply missed—or, at worst, ignored. At least, that was what Amy had thought until
the day she had stopped in his office to chat and spotted
a knowing gleam in his eyes. It was then she realized

that he hadn't been oblivious to what she was doing. He hadn't even purposefully overlooked it. He'd seen every single move she'd made—and he had been amused.

Amy had been rocked back on her heels by that lesson, and after that she'd left Dylan Copeland strictly alone.

No. It was completely insane to think that she'd fallen in love with a man who was so detached that the only thing he felt was ironic amusement that she was making a fool of herself over him.

And yet...

In the past few days, while they'd been working so closely together, everything had changed. Dylan hadn't been detached and amused. He'd really seemed to care about her problems and her goals. He'd worked side by side with her to bail Gavin out of trouble.

And somewhere in the last few days, Amy had let down her guard and taken him into her heart. Admitting it didn't come easily, but it was the only explanation that made every odd piece of the puzzle fit.

No wonder she'd been so annoyed by Sarah Harkness's visit to the showrooms. Amy hadn't just been irritated by the woman's giggle, she'd been jealous of the way she'd hung on Dylan's arm.

No wonder she hadn't wanted Sarah to be the one who bought the George III bed. It was because the woman couldn't have been more obvious about her desire to share it with Dylan.

No wonder she had been so provoked when he had suddenly appeared that night in Mitchell Harlow's apartment. It wasn't because Dylan had intervened to rescue her when she didn't need rescuing. It was because he had done so out of obligation rather than desire. Because he had made it so painfully clear that she shouldn't mistake his interference for affection.

He raised his head and said, "Amy, before this goes any farther—"

Do something fast, Amy ordered herself. She couldn't bear seeing that ironic light in his eyes again, or—worse yet—listening to him explain that a mere kiss meant nothing at all and that she mustn't take him seriously.

She looked up at him, her eyes as wide and innocent as she could manage. "Before *what* goes any farther?"

Dylan seemed taken aback.

She stepped out of his suddenly slackened hold. "Thanks, Dylan, you certainly managed to take my mind off the auction for a minute. Creative distraction, I think they call it—but I didn't realize they teach it in personal-assistant school. You must have gotten an *A*." She put both hands up to smooth her hair. "I must get back downstairs, or the crowd will be getting restless."

She swept out of the office before he had moved.

The lobby was still half full of people milling around, chatting, drinking wine and nibbling hors d'oeuvres from the lavish table near the top of the stairs. In the auction room, bidders were starting to take their seats again. A few had apparently not moved at all during the intermission. Among them, Amy noted, were the pair from *Connoisseur's Choice.*

Belatedly she remembered her intention to get them better seats. Not that being at the back of the room had slowed Eric Dougal down much, she reflected, but she went to make the offer anyway.

Brad Parker, who looked terminally bored, seemed to perk up at the suggestion. But Mr. Dougal shook his head. "I can see just fine from here," he said with a smile. "And I've spent all my mad money already, anyway, so there's no need for me to be any closer to the podium.''

"I hope you'll enjoy your purchase," Amy said.

Eric Dougal laughed. "What a deliciously tactful way to put it, when a man my age buys a bed as big and ostentatious as that one. Don't worry about me, Ms. Sherwood. I'm sure I'll get my money's worth."

Brad caught her eye and rolled his gaze toward the ceiling. What was it he'd told her, when they were discussing the job as roving expert? Something about the publisher getting old and unpredictable. Now he seemed to be implying that Eric Dougal had lost his mind altogether.

She moved toward the front of the room. The music which always played softly during intermission had stopped, and a few last bidders were drifting in to take their seats. She paused beside Mitchell Harlow's aisle seat. "I'm sorry I haven't had a chance to say hello, Mitchell. I'm so glad you came, because there's someone here I want you to meet." She looked around the room. "Though I'm afraid I don't see him just at the moment. It's the autograph expert I was telling you about. He looked at your collection today and he wants to discuss it with you. Perhaps—if you'll stay a few minutes after the auction—the three of us can have a conference."

Mitchell nodded.

Amy thought he looked less than interested. Perhaps if she dangled a little more information, he might be more likely to stick around. "He told me he thinks it's a wonderful collection and would bring even more than I expected at auction. But I'll let him give you the details."

Another nod. He wasn't even looking at her. Puzzled,

Amy followed the direction of his gaze and concluded that he was staring at the back of Honey's head. Just then, as if she'd sensed his rapt attention, Honey turned casually around to survey the crowd. For a moment her profile was perfectly displayed; then her wide-eyed gaze swept over them, lingering for just a moment on Mitchell before moving on.

Poor Mitchell, Amy thought. He seemed to be expert at picking out women who were much more interested in someone else than they could ever be in him.

Which brought Amy face-to-face again with the epiphany she'd experienced up in her office just now. What an idiot she'd been not even to suspect that she was falling for Dylan....

But it was too late to change that. The problem now was what she was going to do about it.

Nothing, she told herself, *except pretend it never happened.* It was the only path she could take, because the last thing she wanted was for Dylan to suspect what a fool she had been. It was bad enough to admit to herself that she had fallen in love with a man who could not have been more up-front and fair about his lack of intentions where she was concerned. But it would be truly unbearable if he realized what she'd done.

The only good thing was that the situation could not go on for much longer. The instant Gavin returned to work—even sooner, if she could manage it—Amy would be gone, and she'd make it a point not to come anywhere near Dylan Copeland again.

In the meantime, she would simply act as if nothing had changed. Even, she thought grimly, if it killed her.

When she parked her car in Carol's driveway, Amy was surprised to see her mother beside the front steps, kneeling in her new flower bed. "Do I have the wrong day?" she called as she started across the lawn. "Tonight is your sorority's charity auction—isn't it?"

Carol sat back on her heels. "If you're afraid I invited you and Dylan to dinner and then forgot all about it—"

"Well, you can't blame me for wondering, when you're out here instead of in the kitchen."

"Dinner's in the oven." She glanced over Amy's shoulder. "Dylan isn't with you?"

"He's coming separately." It had been Amy's suggestion to take two cars, but he'd agreed very quickly, as if he'd been figuring out how to avoid her. Trying to distract her mother from asking why they weren't together, Amy added, "I thought afterward you and I might have a sort of slumber party."

"We haven't had a chance to really talk for a while," Carol said slowly. "But…not tonight, Amy. In fact, I'm not even going to the auction."

Amy frowned. "But why not? It's your sorority. It was your idea for us to do this."

"Something came up. What did you want to talk about that requires a slumber party, anyway?"

"Nothing important, I suppose." *Certainly not Dylan.* She plunged into the first subject that occurred to her. "Gavin was released from the hospital today. I stopped by this morning to tell him about the auction results but he'd already left. And when I called his apartment there was no answer. I suppose Honey dragged him out to go shopping or something." She was babbling and she knew it, but she couldn't seem to stop herself—even though her mother was obviously less than comfortable at hearing all the details.

"How much did the bed bring?" Carol asked suddenly. Her voice was absolutely level, as if she had no personal interest in the answer.

Amy, grateful for the interruption, told her. "It was more than I expected, frankly. And guess who bought it. The publisher of *Connoisseur's Choice*."

"Eric Dougal?"

"You know him?"

"Gavin does. I've just met him at parties, things like that." Carol stood up, dusting dirt off her hands, and picked up her basket.

For the first time Amy noticed the contents—a heap of tiny, fragile, wilted seedlings. She looked from the basket to the flower bed and was alarmed to realize that the earth was bare, the bed empty. Carol had pulled up by the roots every last one of the flowers she had planted so carefully only days before. "Mother," Amy breathed. "What in the name of heaven is wrong with—"

"Oh, there's Dylan now," Carol interrupted. "Which means I only have a minute to tell you."

"Tell me what?" Amy's throat was tight with foreboding.

"Or perhaps I should say, to warn you. You see, dear... Well, you're wrong about one thing. Honey didn't drag Gavin out to shop today, because he's inside."

"Inside what?" Amy said blankly.

"The house. *This* house. He's taking a nap on the couch."

There was one good thing about the bombshell Carol had dropped, Amy realized a good deal later. Her parents—accidentally, it was true, but no less efficiently—had managed to take her mind off Dylan for a while and made it much easier to behave as if that kiss last night had never happened.

"I can't believe it," she told Dylan as they left the house almost two hours later on their way to the sorority auction.

"Which part of it?"

"Everything. For starters, admitting that she went to the hospital intending to give him the sharp edge of her tongue about him selling the bed, but when she saw him lying there surrounded by machines...."

"You have to remember she hadn't seen him at all since he got sick," Dylan pointed out. "He looks a lot better to you and me than he did a few days ago, but compared to what she was used to seeing, he must have seemed pretty frail."

"So she didn't yell at him after all. She just calmly told him how unhappy and how disappointed in him she was, and how unfair he was being."

"I told you she didn't seem to me like a screamer."

Amy was hardly listening. "And because she had come to see him and didn't shriek at him, he worked up his courage to confess all about his financial troubles and how this illness had made him realize that Honey wasn't the loyal kind and that he'd made an enormous mistake and he'd give anything to be able to start over."

"What's so surprising about that? Everybody else knew it—at least about Honey and the size of his mistake—long ago."

"That's my whole point. It was such a huge thing that I'm amazed he admitted it to himself, much less to Mother."

"It was the first time in months that they've come face-to-face in noncombative surroundings. And when the two of them could just talk, with no restrictions and no lawyers—"

"But if all that isn't unlikely enough, the part I really can't believe is that Mother actually agreed to let him have a second chance. And even tore up her new flowerbed because he's allergic to the scent of those particular flowers." Amy looked steadily at him. "You expected this, didn't you? That's why you kept me from going after her that day."

"Oh, no. I'm not that kind of idealist. I told you exactly what I thought at the time—that it would be healthier for everybody if Carol stopped bottling up her feelings. That's all I was hoping for."

"But you said—a long time ago—that the reason she called every day to find out how Gavin was doing was because she was still concerned about him."

"I think I also told you that being concerned is one thing. Wanting him back is another."

Amy frowned. "You don't think she did it—brought him home, I mean—just because she felt sorry for him?"

"Nope. Just don't expect happily-ever-after, Amy. They've got a lot of baggage to work through."

"And a lot of reasons to try to solve the problems."

"They'll make it, I think, if they both really want to try. There are still plenty of sparks there. Or weren't you watching how they looked at each other?"

"Frankly," Amy said, "I didn't even notice. I was too busy imagining the scene this morning when Gavin gave Honey her comeuppance. It seems a little hard on her—losing her trip to Italy and everything—but I suppose that's what she gets for not even going to the hospital to see him every day. At least she had a pleasant evening last night at the auction, dreaming of how she'd spend Eric Dougal's forty thousand dollars." She paused beside her car and folded her arms on the roof, looking across at him. "Speaking of Eric Dougal—"

Dylan was searching his pockets for his keys and didn't look at her. "What about him?"

"Do you think Gavin was just a little too casual when I told him about Mr. Dougal buying the bed?"

"What do you mean, too casual?"

Amy thought he looked uncomfortable, and his expression was all the confirmation she needed. "You know something, don't you? Did Gavin swear you to secrecy?"

"Amy—"

"Never mind, I know you won't answer. You may not be the secretarial type but you can certainly be an oyster about the boss's secrets."

"What are you talking about?"

"The bed. And don't tell me you don't know anything about it. Mother let it slip that Gavin knows Eric Dougal."

"What's surprising about that? They've both been in the antiques trade in this city for years. They must have run across each other."

"No, the way she said it told me it was a lot more than just a casual acquaintance. I'll bet that after Mother and Dad patched it up, Gavin really regretted putting the bed up for sale. He's more sentimental than he wants to admit, or he wouldn't have asked her for it in the first place. And now it's even more nostalgic since it's the thing that brought them back together, too."

"So why didn't he just withdraw it from the sale?"

Amy shook her head. "The average owner could do that, I suppose, but if Gavin did it with his own property it would look like a setup. Auction ethics being what they are, he couldn't pull it out of the sale once it had been advertised. It would have looked as if he'd listed it in the first place just to draw high-class bidders, without any intention of actually selling it. But he couldn't bear to let it go, so he called his friend and asked him to buy the bed back at any price. How much do you want to bet I'm right?"

Dylan shook his head. "I think I'll stand pat. I'm one bottle of champagne down already."

It was a bottle of champagne they would never share, Amy thought, and for an instant the reminder brought all the sadness flooding back. She had to force herself to keep her tone light. "You have no sense of adventure, Copeland. No sporting instincts." She pulled the car door open. "The auction's in the auditorium. I'll see you there."

But Dylan didn't get into his car. "You know, Amy, I don't see why you're so surprised about this."

"Gavin buying back the bed?"

"No. Gavin and Carol getting back together. It's the simplest principle of economics."

"Do you mean that old saying about how two can live more cheaply than one? It might even be true, if one of the pair isn't Honey. But I don't see—"

Dylan was shaking his head. "That's not what I'm talking about. Let's say you borrow money to buy a car."

"Yeah?"

"What happens if you don't pay back the loan?"

"They come and haul away the car. What's that got to do with my parents?"

"He couldn't pay the alimony he owed her," Dylan said gently. "So she just repossessed him."

The college auditorium was more than half full of people, a better showing than Amy had expected for a charity auction. Either Carol's sorority sisters had put together an incredible list of goodies to sell in their fund-raising effort, or they were very good at guilt-tripping their friends into showing up and bidding.

Amy and Dylan were shown to seats at the side of the stage, near a long row of tables heaped with merchandise and brown envelopes, each item neatly numbered. ''There's a master list,'' the sorority president explained. ''One of our members—her name's Ruth—will be along any minute to assist. She put the list together and is familiar with all the items, so if a description isn't clear or someone in the audience has a question, Ruth will be happy to explain it. We're not being very formal here tonight.''

''Not very formal?'' Amy murmured as the woman moved away. ''I haven't seen so many diamonds in one room since the Candlelight Ball last autumn. We need to decide how we'll split this up. Every other item?'' A sudden movement from the edge of the stage caught her attention. ''Oh, no,'' she whispered. ''This must be Ruth.''

''What's the matter?''

''Ruth's last name is Maxwell,'' Amy groaned.

Dylan turned casually to take a look. ''You mean the Mrs. Maxwell of Picasso fame?''

''That's the one. She can't have known about the change in auctioneers, or I'll bet she'd have found a way to excuse herself. This is not going to be pretty.''

Ruth Maxwell perched on the edge of the chair next to Amy. ''Thank you for sending the lovely roses, Ms. Sherwood.''

The woman sounded a bit chilly, which was a great deal better than if she'd been frothing at the mouth, Amy thought. "I can't begin to tell you how sorry I am for the misunderstanding, Mrs. Maxwell."

"And I can't begin to apologize for my husband's behavior."

Amy tried in vain to keep her jaw from dropping.

"It was very noble of you to take the blame," Ruth Maxwell went on, "but the flowers and your note of apology made him feel so guilty about it that he finally confessed what had happened. It's the usual story—I suppose you're well-accustomed to hearing it. He's suffered some reverses in the stock market, and he'd made a couple of loans to friends who now can't repay them."

"Told you so," Dylan breathed into Amy's ear.

"In short, we will be selling the Picasso after all, Ms. Sherwood. We'd be grateful if you'd overlook our earlier contretemps and work with us."

Amy managed to say, "I'd be happy to."

"Then I'll be in touch about a time when we can meet to discuss the details." She looked around. "I see someone has rearranged the merchandise—I'd better straighten it out or we'll be confused all evening." She moved over to the tables.

"Congratulations," Dylan said softly. "So much for your fear of failure."

"But you can't really call getting the Picasso my success," Amy protested. "It sort of happened in spite of me."

"You made a good investment in roses, I'd say. With the kind of record you're building up, Gavin will be in tears if you leave."

"He'll just have to deal with it. I've made up my mind."

"Sure about that? I thought your main reason for leaving the auction house was Honey. But now that she's out of the picture—''

For a moment, Amy had completely forgotten saying anything of the sort. But Dylan was right—not only had Gavin's affair with Honey been her reason for leaving originally, but the woman had served as a handy excuse for Amy's determination to get away from Sherwood Auctions again as soon as she possibly could. But now that Honey was no longer a factor...

Amy realized with chagrin how very neatly she had boxed herself in. She couldn't stay, because that would mean continuing to work with Dylan—but she certainly couldn't admit that he was the reason she didn't want to stay.

She tried to dodge the question. ''I don't know what I'll do. Everything has changed so much, and so suddenly. I'll have to think it over.''

''Gavin will be unhappy if you leave.''

''That won't be anything new. And Brad Parker and Eric Dougal wouldn't be exactly thrilled with me if I backed out now—after they've held the roving expert job for me at the magazine.''

Dylan let the silence draw out. ''So what do you want to do?''

Stay at the auction house, Amy thought. *With you. But only if you want me not just as a partner in work, but in everything.*

And, since she absolutely could not have that—

She couldn't begin to explain. Maybe by tomorrow, when she'd had a chance to think and to construct a story that would hold together, she could answer him—and convince herself.

It was odd, she thought. Only when it had seemed for a moment that she could once more have her job at the

auction house—and then realized she couldn't after all—
had she truly understood how much she wanted to stay.
Once *Connoisseur's Choice* had been everything she
hoped for, the job as roving expert the pinnacle of her
dreams. Now it came in a very poor second.

A second she would have to live with.

The president of the organization was speaking, intro-
ducing them. Amy heard her name and walked across
the stage to the podium. Ruth Maxwell handed her a big,
thick brown envelope.

Amy looked at the typed description and said, "Our
first item this evening is a weekend of shows and casino
play in Las Vegas, retail value five thousand dollars. Do
I have an opening bid?"

Ruth Maxwell apparently felt that a decision once made
should be carried out as promptly as possible, for she
called Amy on Sunday morning and asked her to stop
by before midday. "Now that we've faced the necessity
of selling," she said, "we'd rather not drag out the pain.
So we'd like to make the arrangements as soon as possible."

The meeting was brief and businesslike, and Amy was
on her way out of the apartment tower in less than half
an hour, with a signed contract naming Sherwood
Auctions as the agent to sell the Maxwells' Picasso and
an agreement to have a crew pick up the painting on
Monday.

She stopped at the security desk to make arrangements
for a couple of her staff to be admitted the following
day in order to crate and move the painting. While the
guard was filling out the papers, Amy's gaze wandered,
focusing finally on a name at the bottom of the visitors'
list. *Brad Parker to see Mr. Dougal.*

So this was where Eric Dougal lived. Not surprising that he'd choose the most exclusive building in the city.

The guard pushed the papers across to her, and Amy reached for a pen. Just then a woman came up beside her and rapped on the desk to get the guard's attention. "I'm Miss Lambert, and I'm here to see Mr. Harlow," she said impatiently.

Amy turned her head so quickly her neck popped. "Honey?"

Honey's eyes narrowed. "Since I don't have to be polite to you anymore, Amy *darling,* I'm sure you'll understand why I don't stand around and chat."

The guard flipped back a page of the visitors' list to check. "You can go on up," he said and added, as Honey disappeared into the elevator, "Whew. Mr. Harlow picked himself a real winner there."

"Maybe she chose him instead." Amy was remembering the night of the auction and recalling how, while she and Mitchell had been talking about his autograph collection, Honey had just happened to turn around and make fleeting eye contact with him. Now Amy wasn't so sure it had been a coincidence. She'd been careful of what she said, because of the crowded room. Still, if Honey had overheard even a bit of that conversation and drawn some shrewd conclusions...

She was working on alternatives even before Gavin dumped her, Amy realized. *I may not have done Mitchell any favor by telling him those autographs are worth a fortune.*

But her business was selling merchandise, Amy reminded herself. It wasn't up to her to police what the client did with the proceeds of the sale. In any case, by the time Mitchell's autographs produced any cash for him, Amy would be gone from the auction house and none of it would be any of her business.

Maybe, by then, she'd even be happy about her choice.

She turned away from the desk just as the elevator door opened and a group of men came out into the lobby. Eric Dougal and Brad Parker—that combination was reasonable, of course, even if it would have made more sense for them to meet on a business day at the magazine's headquarters. And it was not even surprising, since she'd seen Brad's name on the visitors' list.

But why was Dylan with them? And he was unmistakably part of the group, because Eric Dougal was holding the leash of an excitable Irish setter—Dylan's dog, Reggie, who whined and tugged when she saw Amy.

"We'll expect you on board sometime this week then," Brad said to Dylan, and held out a hand. "As soon as you can cut yourself loose from this adventure at the auction house. If I hadn't heard the story myself, I wouldn't believe it. Unless Mr. Dougal wants to do it himself, it'll be my pleasure to introduce you around the office as our new—"

Amy stepped forward. "Roving expert?" she asked politely. "I don't suppose I should be surprised, Dylan, since I told you about the job myself. No wonder you've been trying to convince me that I should stay at the auction house. It would have left the field free for you— except you didn't even wait that long, did you?"

Dylan winced. Brad looked blank. Eric Dougal pursed his lips as if to whistle.

"No, Amy," Dylan said. "Roving expert is still your job, if you want it."

She felt like a fool. "But then—"

He didn't answer. The silence drew out.

Eric Dougal said, "Dylan will be taking my place as publisher of *Connoisseur's Choice*. It's what he came to Kansas City to do. What I raised him to do, if it comes to that. Well, my boy? Don't you think you should officially introduce this young lady to your grandfather?"

CHAPTER TEN

IT HAD never occurred to Dylan to wonder how a shish kabab felt as it was taken off the grill, neatly skewered and singed on the edges. Now he knew. Amy's eyes were hotter than any barbecue and sharper than any skewer ever made. And the way she was looking at him left him definitely feeling singed—and not just on the edges.

He didn't ignore his grandfather's request; he simply didn't hear it. He took a step toward Amy.

Eric Dougal looked from one to the other. "Perhaps we'll make it official another time," he said, sounding sympathetic. Tipping his hat to Amy, he let the Irish setter pull him toward the door. Brad Parker went with him, though he looked back over his shoulder a couple of times as if he'd like to stay and see the show.

"I wanted to tell you." To his own ears his voice sounded hoarse, and even as Dylan said the words, he knew how horribly inadequate they were.

"Tell me what?" Amy's voice was low and fierce. "That you've been spying?"

He was taken aback. What had made her jump to that conclusion? "No!"

"Can we look forward to some kind of exposé of Sherwood Auctions in the pages of *Connoisseur's Choice?* What have we supposedly been doing? Selling stolen property? Illegally importing antiquities?"

"No," he said firmly. "Gavin may have done some

crazy things in his personal life, but his business ethics are the cleanest anywhere around. You know that.''

''Then why have you been hiding out?''

He hesitated. ''I've been sort of investigating the auction business in general.''

It was obvious she'd noted the hesitation. *''Sort of?''*

''Learning about antiques and collectibles. It was the best way to—''

''What a comfort that will be to Gavin when he finds out about you,'' Amy mocked. ''To find out that he hasn't been your target, just your patsy.''

''Gavin knows exactly what I've been doing. He's known from the beginning.''

She pulled back as if he'd slapped her. Dylan felt as if he had.

''Thank you very much for your confidence in me,'' she said bitterly.

''Nobody knew, Amy. Just Gavin and my grandfather.'' He was making things worse, because she was obviously in no mood to be receptive. But giving up wasn't an option; he had to keep trying. ''Listen to me. At first there was no reason to tell you—you weren't even working directly with your father, so there was absolutely no need for you to know. Then, by the time Gavin put you in charge, you had so many other things on your mind that I couldn't see adding to your problems.''

''Are you sure that was the reason? Or did you just decide not to shut off a great source of information? I must have sounded like a babbling brook, telling you all about Gavin's financial troubles and the divorce—''

''None of that is going to show up in the magazine.''

''Only because it turned out to be nothing. I trusted you, Dylan!''

"And you still can."

She stared at him, openmouthed. "I suppose you think I should just take your word for it? After you've lied to me—"

"I didn't lie, Amy."

"Only because you didn't have to. It never occurred to me to ask, 'Hey, Dylan, are you really a reporter in disguise?' I'd have been just as likely to wonder whether you were an astronaut, or a brain surgeon taking a vacation!"

"I was there for information all right," he admitted, "but not the kind that would hurt the auction house in any way."

"And while you were gathering it, you did everything you could to make sure I didn't suspect what you really were. You called *Connoisseur's Choice* a stuffy magazine!"

"It is, a bit," he said thoughtfully. "That's one of the—"

"Stop trying to change the subject!"

She was almost yelling, and a matron who was crossing the lobby looked down her long nose at them.

Dylan said, "Look, let's go somewhere quieter and talk about this."

"Am I embarrassing you, Dylan? What a pity. But I'm not going anywhere with you, because there isn't anything to talk about." She turned on her heel, and then looked back at him. "You might do me a favor and tell Brad I've had second thoughts about being a roving expert. I'm not taking the job."

He could hardly say that was a surprise, though he couldn't help but wonder if her decision was really as sudden as it seemed. If it was...if she had turned down the job solely because she was furious with him....

He said, almost tentatively, "I suspected you'd decide in the end that you'd rather stay at the auction company."

"Oh, you're quite right, but that's beside the point. I'd rather work anywhere you're not. And by the way— don't feel you have to pretend to be a personal assistant any more. You can start your new job tomorrow, because you've done a great job—how did Brad phrase it?—of cutting yourself loose from your great adventure at the auction house."

She marched across the lobby and was gone before he could move.

It took a while for Amy's head to clear enough for her to think straight, and even then she wasn't sure she'd got all the facts lined up correctly in her mind. But a couple of things had suddenly become plain. No wonder Gavin hadn't turned his business over to Dylan to run. And no wonder Dylan had kept insisting he didn't want Gavin's job. They'd both known he had a better one waiting for him.

But what little he'd told her still didn't explain why Dylan had been in hiding.

I've been investigating the auction business in general. I was there for information.

None of that was very helpful. Of course, it really didn't matter much to her, whatever his reasons had been. The important thing where Amy was concerned was that he'd had every opportunity to confide in her, but he hadn't.

That didn't necessarily mean that whatever he was up to was criminal—or even shady. But it certainly told her that he hadn't considered it vital that she know what was going on.

She wasn't important enough to him to be considered at all—and that was what hurt her worst. It had been difficult enough for Amy to admit that she'd made the enormous mistake of falling in love with a man who didn't return her affection. But the blow of finding that even the working partnership she had treasured hadn't been real—that it had been based not on trust but on half-truths piled on a base of sand—was harder still to bear.

Amy paused for a full fifteen seconds on the sidewalk, looking up at the block-square building that housed Sherwood Auctions, before she took a deep breath and pulled open the main door. It was early yet, and the reception area was quiet. Robert was at the desk, just answering a call, and Beth Gleason stood nearby, checking her watch and tapping her fingertips on the counter. The chairs in the waiting room were empty.

"On your way to the Battling Bensons again?" Amy asked.

Beth nodded. "I'm waiting for the rest of the team. If we go as a group, the weird sisters tend to leave us alone, but regardless of their agreement, pity the poor appraiser who gets isolated from the crowd."

"How's it going?"

"Faster than I expected, considering the way we started out. We should be finished late this week."

Robert punched a button and looked across the desk at Amy. "This call is for you. Want me to put it through upstairs?"

She shook her head. "It'll take me too long to get up there." She reached for the phone, but as soon as she heard Dylan's voice on the other end of the line, she regretted answering. She didn't bother with preliminaries. "If you're calling to ask how Gavin is, I don't know. Why not phone Mother? She can pay you back for all the reporting you did to her."

"I'm calling to finish our conversation from yesterday."

"There's nothing else to say. Besides, I'm very busy."

"You'll be spending the day supervising the crew as they set up the showroom displays for the next auction."

"My goodness," she said with mock surprise, "you *did* pay attention while you were here."

"I tried to call you after you walked out on me yesterday."

"I didn't walk out on you. I left because I'd finished everything I wanted to say."

"Maybe you had. But I hadn't."

"That's not my problem."

"I didn't want to bother you at work."

"Then why are you calling?" Amy asked sweetly. "Not that you're going to bother me for long, because I'm hanging up."

"I wouldn't be phoning you now, except that your cell phone didn't seem to be working yesterday."

"Imagine that. Must be something wrong with the circuits. I'll have it checked over—sometime next month, maybe."

She was handing the telephone back to Robert when she heard Dylan say, "Have you forgotten that I still owe you a bottle of champagne?"

She put the receiver back to her ear. "As a matter of fact, I had. How kind of you to remind me. Tell you what, Dylan. Don't bother with Dom Pérignon. Just buy the cheapest brand you can find, in the heaviest bottle.

Then hit yourself over the head with it and consider the lump my final word on the subject."

"Amy—"

"Furthermore, for your information, I'll be hiring a real personal assistant, and believe me, part of his or her job will be to answer my telephone. So you might as well not bother calling back."

She dropped the receiver on the counter with a bang.

Robert was staring at her in disbelief.

Beth said mildly, "Had a squabble, hmm?"

Amy held her head high. "Buzz me in, please, Robert. I want to get started. It's going to be a long day."

As she went through into the lobby, she heard him mutter, "You can say that again."

The mansion on Ward Parkway gleamed in the early afternoon sun as Amy parked her car in the driveway, and a soft breeze teased her hair as she approached the front door. The house looked quiet, peaceful and inviting—and if that wasn't a mirage, Amy thought, she had never seen one. For this was the day when the Battling Bensons would decide which of them ended up with the prized Meissen china, the gothic chair, the silver tea service, and every other item on fifty single-spaced pages of the inventory Beth Gleason's team had produced in more than two weeks of intensive work.

It was the first time Amy had come to the mansion without Dylan, and despite the lecture she'd given herself as she drove across Kansas City, memories were swarming around her like irritated yellow jackets. An amazing number of memories, she thought, considering that they'd only visited the house twice.

Recollections of the two of them speculating over lunch about what Mrs. Benson's "odds and ends" might include. Of making the champagne bet and Dylan saying, with their first glance inside the front door, that he preferred Dom Pérignon. Of Hattie bursting in and Dylan by sheer strength of personality forcing the stepsiblings to see reason...

She remembered noticing the easy way he had exerted his authority that day. But—distracted by the Battling Bensons—she had shrugged it off rather than following the thought to its natural conclusion. Why hadn't it occurred to her that he must be used to command, because it obviously came so automatically to him?

She rang the bell and watched the traffic speeding along Ward Parkway as she waited for Thomas the butler to answer. Now that it was too late to change her mind, she almost wished she had brought Beth along today, just to have a little moral support. But Beth was already plunging into her next big job, getting ready for an auction of china figurines next month. And—even more to the point—Beth had a nasty habit of seeing things too clearly. Especially things that Amy would just as soon keep in the dark.

Still, facing the Fearsome Foursome by herself was not an inviting prospect. She could handle them as long as they were quarreling with one another. But if they ever made up their differences, they'd be a force to be reckoned with.

Of course, the Battling Bensons combining resources was as unlikely a scenario as Dylan showing up at the auction house to throw himself at her feet and declare that his life was worthless without her.

And that, Amy told herself, was quite enough of that sort of nonsense.

She was beginning to think that the assorted siblings had stood her up altogether when the front door finally creaked open and the butler peered out, then without a word ushered her through the front hall and into the dining room.

The room was quiet, but the cluttered table made it apparent that at least some of the siblings had already arrived. The top of it was littered with briefcases and notebooks, copies of the inventory, dozens of pens and sharpened pencils, pads of sticky notes, and an adding machine.

A big, old-fashioned, probably noisy, and certainly intimidating adding machine. Who, she wondered, had brought that?

Her gaze flicked around the room and came to rest on the only occupant, who was standing beside the hutch full of cheap pottery at the far end of the room.

Dylan.

Amy's first reaction was a surge of pure pleasure, but it was quickly mingled with pain as she realized how vulnerable she was—and how foolish she had been to hope that time and separation would make it all easier to bear. If simply seeing him could send such a torrent of emotion through her, then the two weeks of his absence from the auction house had done nothing at all to heal her.

Perhaps, she thought, nothing ever would.

She tried to regain both her poise and her command of the situation. "What are you doing here?"

"You should probably ask Hattie, since she was the one who asked me to come."

"Well, since Hattie's not here, I'm asking you."

"She told me she hoped you wouldn't be offended, but—"

"I didn't think she knew the meaning of the word.

Don't feel you have to sugarcoat this, Dylan. Give it to me straight.''

''All right. She said the Bensons not only have trouble trusting each other but they find it difficult to believe that any one individual can truly be impartial and objective in a matter that's as large and complex as this one.''

''Even though this auction was my idea in the first place.''

''I'm only telling you what she said. Since I've been involved from the beginning they thought I should be here for the finale, too, just as a sort of balance wheel to make sure you don't take sides.''

''The Fearsome Foursome actually agree on something? That's incredible—even if it's just that they don't have confidence in me.'' She looked around. ''Where are they all, anyway?''

Dylan ticked them off on his fingers. ''Sylvia brought the adding machine, but the cord isn't long enough to reach the outlet so she went to look for an extension. When Emma saw the adding machine, she decided she'd better have a calculator of some sort, too, so Sylvia couldn't get the best of her by manipulating the numbers, so she took off for Brookside to buy one.''

''You know,'' Amy mused, ''I'm not the least offended that they don't trust me. It positively makes me feel like one of the family.''

She thought Dylan was biting back a smile. It annoyed her to think that he was actually enjoying himself, that he hadn't even seemed to notice she was miserable. Not that she wanted him to notice, she added hastily, because if he did, and starting thinking about why she was so unhappy…the consequences didn't bear thinking about.

Dylan went on, ''Hattie is upstairs making sure that the items she's planning to bid on are still in mint condition, and Bill is in the kitchen. He mumbled something about needing a drink.''

''I don't blame him. In fact, I feel like joining him. Foolish me—I was hoping that the fact they could all agree on a time to do this meant there was hope for them.''

She pulled out the chair at the head of the table and opened her briefcase. ''I even brought my gavel,'' she said. ''Something tells me I'll need it to maintain order with this crowd.''

Dylan didn't seem to be listening. ''Amy,'' he began softly. ''I was going to tell you about the magazine the night of the furniture auction.''

She didn't look at him. ''Of course, we only have your word for that, don't we? To say nothing of the fact that you had a hundred opportunities before then and you missed every one of them. So why don't we just agree that this is a pointless conversation and not go to the bother of talking?''

''Because we have time to kill.''

''True,'' she admitted. ''Let's see, what could we talk about instead? Oh, I'll bet you can't guess where my parents are right now.''

''Italy?''

''Not quite. That's where they're headed, but they decided to go by cruise ship so Gavin will have plenty of time to rest. Mother put her foot down. And when he gets back, he'll be working part-time only.''

''And you'll be in charge? That's what he always wanted, Amy.'' He paused, and then said softly, ''But the real question is what you want. Did you give up the roving expert job because of me?''

She looked at him very levelly. ''No, Dylan.''

''If that's the truth,'' he mused, ''then what did you

mean when you said you'd rather work anywhere than with me?''

''I hope you don't think you deserve an answer to that.''

''I intend to get one,'' he said quietly.

The dining-room doors burst open, and Emma and Sylvia came in, one brandishing a calculator still in its plastic wrappings, the other dragging a thick yellow extension cord, and both talking loudly and irritably. Drawn by the noise they made, Bill Benson came in from the kitchen with a highball glass in his hand, and a couple of minutes later Hattie clattered down the stairs and took her seat.

''Let's get this over with,'' Hattie said.

Bill's voice was a little blurry. ''The sooner the better.''

Amy tapped her gavel. ''Item one, a Staffordshire china shepherdess. Does everyone know which one we're talking about?''

Only once did she have to bang her gavel to bring order. When she reminded them that if they didn't settle to business they'd still be at it when dawn broke, the four of them looked at each other with distaste, settled back into their chairs, and stopped shouting.

Three hours later it was over, except that Sylvia's adding machine was still rattling as she added up the final tallies. It sounded like an old-fashioned stock ticker that had been crossed with a Gatling gun. Finally she sat back from the table, looking bewildered. ''I don't believe it,'' she said. ''The total bids—each person's total, I mean—ended up almost identical.''

Amy couldn't resist. ''I told you it would be the fairest way to divide everything.''

The siblings trailed out. As Sylvia and Emma vanished into the hall, Amy heard one of them say, "If you want to borrow the Meissen sometime—for a dinner party or something—just ask."

She could hardly believe her ears. "And nobody even shed blood," she muttered. She eyed Dylan, still sitting at the table. "Don't let me keep you. I've still got to sort out the list of what's left over—what none of them wanted—so the crew from the auction house can pick it all up tomorrow." She bent her head over her copy of the inventory to translate her scrawled notes before she forgot what each marking meant.

"You'll have to let me know when the framed jigsaw puzzles go up for sale," Dylan murmured. He was looking at the thousand-piece art reproduction hanging on the wall above Amy's head. "I've developed quite a fondness for Venus on the half-shell, there."

"I'll make sure you get it."

But still he didn't move.

Finally, exasperated, she said, "Don't you have something you need to do, Dylan?"

"Yes. Talk to you."

"And you're going to sit here and stare at me till I listen?" She threw her pencil down. "Fine. Get it over with."

He let the silence draw out for a long moment, as if he was figuring out how to start. Then he leaned forward and folded his arms on the table. "I've worked on magazines all my life," he said. "The way you learned the auction business, I learned publishing. It's what my family does, and I know it backward. We've got thirty magazines, and I've been on staff at all of them—except *Connoisseur's Choice*."

Amy frowned.

He seemed to see her question before it was entirely

formed. "That one has always been my grandfather's personal baby. He's kept it separate from the rest of the chain, handled it personally, made it uniquely his. I never thought he'd retire. Nobody did. But last fall he called me out here and told me he was getting tired, and he wanted to turn the magazine over to me. I was his logical replacement, he said. The one who thought the most like he did." He smiled a little. "I'm not sure that was a compliment. But he was determined that it never be run as just another magazine. So as a condition for his bowing out, he insisted that I had to know as much about antiques before I took over as I know about magazines."

Amy shrugged. "Sounds reasonable to me. *Connoisseur's Choice* is unique—even the people who work in the mail room must get questions about what's valuable these days."

"Yes," he said slowly. "The problem is that it isn't as easy to learn about antiques as you'd think."

"If the field wasn't so large and complex, there wouldn't be a need for a magazine."

"But it's even more than that, Amy. There's an awful lot to learn, yes. But to make it more complicated, the moment people find out you're connected with a magazine, they either want to impress you or cover something up. Besides, the kind of understanding my grandfather insisted on doesn't come from talking to people as a reporter does, anyway. That's too casual and too easy. Too shallow. The only way to learn it was to live with it—but I didn't have a lifetime to do it, the way he did."

"So whose idea was it for you to work at the auction house?"

"Gavin's, I think. He was the only person my grandfather confided in. What better way to learn, he said, than to work for a while in the auction business, where I'd see a little of everything. You said yourself the wide experience you've had at Sherwood's made you the perfect roving expert for the magazine.''

''That, and a degree in design and art appreciation, and a couple of decades of practice.''

''I grant you that. The trouble was I didn't have even the minimal qualifications for any regular job at the auction house. Imagine if he'd put me in the china section as an assistant appraiser.''

Amy could picture the scene with absolutely no trouble. ''Beth Gleason would have been in his face screaming about him hiring people with no training or experience.''

''And who could blame her? Besides, the uproar would have drawn attention to me. That's when Gavin thought of the personal assistant gig. I would be perfectly placed to see everything that was going on, every item that came through the auction process. Besides, I'd be right at his elbow to be tutored, but nobody would question why I was being singled out for that kind of special training.''

''No wonder you didn't make his phone calls or photocopies,'' Amy muttered.

''I told you I wasn't a secretary.'' He stood up and began to pace the room. ''Whatever you think, I wasn't hiding, Amy. I mean, I didn't change my name, and I didn't create a false history. I didn't have to. Since Gavin so clearly accepted me, so did everyone else. And it was part of the arrangement that nobody else knew. I think my grandfather intended it as a sort of test—he wanted to see if I could make it without the boost that my magazine connections would give me. But his insistence on my staying undercover meant that to some extent I was living a lie—you were right about that. And because of that, I couldn't allow myself to be attracted to you.''

''Cute excuse,'' she said. ''You should get a patent on it.'' But something had clutched at her throat. Probably, she thought, it was the fear that once more she would get her hopes up only to see them smashed.

''That worked all right,'' he mused, ''as long as you were just flitting into the office from time to time. Though I didn't realize until you were gone how much I'd enjoyed having you around.''

Her heart skipped a beat, but she told herself not to be naive. *He probably just missed all the fun of watching me make a fool of myself.*

''Then Gavin got sick, and circumstances threw us together,'' he went on, ''and I found I couldn't keep my distance. I tried, because it wouldn't have been fair to you, when you didn't know the whole story.''

So this whole conversation was really about fairness, she thought. She'd accused him of lying to her, and he'd thought it over and felt guilty because he hadn't told her the whole truth. That was all. He hadn't mentioned caring about her, or even being particularly attracted to her. He'd just said that he'd found it difficult to keep his distance while working in the same office. Whatever that meant. *Treat it lightly, Amy.*

''So now I know,'' she said. She pushed back her chair and stood up. ''Thanks for telling me everything. At least, I assume that's everything?'' It was a throw-away line; she'd handed it to him deliberately so he didn't have to search for an excuse to get up and leave.

''No, that's not everything.'' Dylan turned to face her. ''You don't know what I was going to tell you that night after the furniture auction, when I followed you to your office.''

Amy frowned. ''You said you were going to tell me about the magazine.''

''Yes. But there was more.'' He took a deep breath. ''If you'd given me the chance, I would have confessed what I'd been trying for days not to admit to myself. That somewhere along the way you'd gotten to be more than the boss's daughter, or even the boss. A whole lot more.''

Before this goes any farther, he'd said that night, and so, leaping to the conclusion that he was trying to let her down gently, she had ended it herself. The realization of what she'd done made everything around Amy suddenly look a peculiar, sickly orange.

''I'd fallen in love with you. With your loyalty, and your courage, and your honesty. With every bit of you.''

Amy's throat was so tight she couldn't make a sound.

''It really shook me up the night I walked into Mitchell Harlow's apartment and found him kissing you. I could have cheerfully throttled him. And you, too, when you made it sound as if you'd sleep with him to get that auction.''

Amy shook her head.

''I know—but you gave me a bad minute in the parking lot. Even when I finally admitted to myself what I was feeling, I had to face the fact that you didn't feel the same way. You obviously didn't care at all. Or at least I thought it was obvious—until you told me that you'd rather work anywhere I wasn't. It was a back-handed sort of comment, but it made me think. If I was important enough that you wanted to avoid me....''

''That's for sure,'' she said. Her voice was small. ''I'd have done anything to get away from you—I'd have even given up the auction house if you'd stayed—because I couldn't bear to be around you, knowing that you didn't care whether I was there or not. Believing that you were perfectly aware I was attracted to you, but you just thought it was amusing. That—''

But she couldn't talk anymore, for she was in his arms and he was kissing her with the passionate intensity they had only begun to find on the night of the auction.

It was a long time later before Amy could breathe again, and begin to think clearly. ''You know,'' she said finally, ''I don't believe I was ever completely fooled. For one thing, I had this nagging feeling that you couldn't be telling the truth when you said you didn't want Gavin's job. You weren't the sort not to be ambitious, not to want responsibility and authority. The two things didn't fit—your personality and the job you were holding, I mean. But I was too busy to think about it, so I just pushed it aside.''

He smiled and kissed her again, and Amy decided there were much better ways to spend her energy than in explaining something which didn't matter anymore.

''Let's send your parents a telegram,'' he murmured. ''I hope they'll be pleased.''

''About getting a telegram?'' Amy asked as innocently as she could. ''I suppose it would be fun, on board the ship. And a little unusual, too. But—''

He slanted a chiding look at her. ''No, my darling. About the idea that we'll be shacking up together as soon as we can find a place to live. That will be a problem, you know. I've been staying with my grandfather.''

''No wonder your name wasn't on the visitors' list that night I went to see Mitchell Harlow,'' Amy mused. ''So much for using your native charm to get past the security guard—you were already in the building.''

Dylan nodded. "I just walked up a few flights. Anyway, I haven't got a place to call my own, and your apartment isn't big enough, so—"

"You haven't even seen my apartment."

"I don't have to," he said patiently. "You told me yourself it was too small for the George III bed."

"But..." Amy's head was spinning. "*You* bought it?" she said faintly. "I thought my parents were just too busy getting ready for their trip to bother having it hauled back to the house. It's still sitting in the shipping department."

"It had better still be sitting there," he said, "considering what I paid for it. And that's the last time I'll turn my grandfather loose with my checkbook, too. Raising the bid by six thousand dollars when you'd already started to drop the gavel.... He thought it was amusing."

"It was a silly, sentimental thing to do," she said. "And I love you for it—along with a lot of other reasons."

"You'll have to give me the whole list sometime," he murmured. "But we can't just let the bed sit in shipping forever. We'll have to look for a house where it will fit." He looked around the dining room with a speculative gleam in his eyes. "What about this one? It'll be for sale."

Amy choked. "After all we've been through—and managed to survive—you actually want to try to negotiate a real estate deal with the Fearsome Foursome?"

He grinned. "It wouldn't be my first choice, no. But that wasn't why I suggested it. You do realize, don't you, that you just agreed we're looking for a house together?"

Amy thought he was stretching the point, but she decided it really didn't matter. "I'm going to ask one last time,'' she said. ''Are there any other secrets I need to know?''

''No. Wait—yes. But only one.''

She pulled back a bit so she could study his face. ''Let me have it.''

''It wasn't exactly Hattie's idea for me to come today. She thinks it was, but—''

Amy shook her head. ''You're too Machiavellian to be running around loose.''

''So do the world a favor, and tie me down.''

''My pleasure,'' Amy murmured. ''Oh, yes. About that bottle of champagne you still owe me—''

''Let's make it a couple of cases,'' Dylan suggested. ''And we'll share it with our wedding guests as soon as your parents get home.''

Strong and silent…
Powerful and passionate…
Tough and tender…

Who can resist the rugged loners of the Outback?
As tough and untamed as the land they rule, they
burn as hot as the Australian sun once they meet
the woman they've been waiting for!

Feel the Outback heat throughout 2002 when
these fabulous authors

Margaret Way
Barbara Hannay
Jessica Hart

bring you:

Men who turn your whole world upside down!

Makes any time special ®

Visit us at www.eHarlequin.com

HRTA